The City of the Old Gods

The Swords of El Cid

By

Robert E. Waters

Dedication
For my sister, Susan Eileen Conder

THE SWORDS OF EL CID

By Robert E Waters

The Swords of El Cid
By Robert E. Waters
Cover image by Dobrosław Wierzbowski
Cover design by Jan Kostka
Zmok Books an imprint of
Winged Hussar Publishing, LLC, 1525 Hulse Road, Unit 1, Point Pleasant, NJ 08742

This edition published in 2020 Copyright ©Winged Hussar Publishing, LLC

ISBN 978-1-94543-013-8 Paperback
ISBN 978-1-95042-334-7 E-book
Library of Congress No. 2020935997

Bibliographical references and index
1. Fantasy 2. Epic Fantasy 3. Action & Adventure

For more information on Winged Hussar Publishing, LLC,
visit us at: https://www.WingedHussarPublishing.com
Twitter: WingHusPubLLC
Facebook: Winged Hussar Publishing LLC

Preface

March 1502 AD, Lübeck, in the German state of Schleswig-Holstein

Georg Cromer, leader of the Hanseatic League, greeted the envoy with rapt indifference. It was what a leader was supposed to do: feign interest in whoever came into his office so that his "subjects" gathered round would think any message or event, no matter how slight, energized and excited their leader. It was a way to keep workers engaged and attentive, and the wolves at bay. It was a game that royalty played, and one that Georg had mastered in his time in Lübeck. But he was no royal man. He was a merchant. A merchant on a mission to save the world.

"Thank you, Peter," he said, accepting the folded note from the stooped man with a curt acknowledgment. "Your dedication to the League will not go unnoticed."

Georg fished around in his vest pocket and found a silver thaler. He thumbed it through the air to Peter, who snatched it greedily and scurried out of the room before he was noticed further. Georg didn't bother opening the note and reading it. He knew what the message contained.

"Is it from our intrepid Catherine of Aragon?" Jacobus Knoblauch, second to Georg, asked in a manner that suggested mild frustration.

Georg chuckled. "That's one way to describe her. No, the letter is not from her. It's about her."

"She is in Spain as ordered?"

Georg shook his head again. "Avignon, France. Or will be soon. We have eyes on her."

"Avignon? Why?"

It was a good question, with only one answer. Georg sighed again. "She is going there to speak to the Teutonic knight's family. To tell them what has happened to their husband, their father. Try to, at least. And she does not travel alone."

"Bah!" Jacobus spit his frustration, and again, Georg shared in it. "With all humility and respect, sir, using Catherine on this mission is a mistake, especially now that she travels with a Saracen. We should order her to return to Lübeck at once and reintroduce her to her obligation to the League. She's too headstrong, too disrespectful of your authority. Too…"

"Willful?"

Jacobus nodded. "Yes."

It was true, and many men, like Jacobus, had difficulty accepting such behavior from a woman, and in Catherine's case, a girl. But she was no regular girl, Georg knew. She was the daughter of King Ferdinand II and Queen Isabella of Spain. That alone afforded her more levity.

But how much?

Georg rose and walked to the window. He stared out at the light snow falling on the Free City, giving it a calm, peaceful visage that he found most comforting. He smiled; despite the urgency of the conversation he was having with his second. Lübeck was his home now and far away from all the epicenters of the fight against the Eldar Gods and their insatiable desire to reclaim the earth for whatever nefarious purposes they had. The events that had transpired recently in East Prussia, in the ruins of that cursed city, Starybogow, had made the League's current mission in Spain all the more dire. And indeed, was Catherine of Aragon the right person to head up that mission? Yes, in some ways. She was a daughter from the most prominent Spanish family. She could work nearly unimpeded throughout Spain, if she were smart enough to use her name and influence to gain access where needed. Was she that smart? Fortunately, yes. But Jacobus, unfortunately, was right: working with a Saracen in Spain, and so soon after the Reconquista, changed the odds of the mission. Time was running out. Pieces on the board were moving fast in Egypt.

Tizona needed to be found… and soon.

Georg turned from the window and stared at Jacobus. "Avignon is just a small delay. Then Catherine will be back on her mission. I'll see to it. I shall have one of our French merchants from Paris deliver my orders to her personally. She will do her duty."

"And if she fails, sir?"

Jacobus's question had a dread about it, and Georg understood the warning quite well. The Eldar Gods were constantly working to breach the distance between this world and their own, but monsters also lay in wait in the Hanseatic League. Georg fought to save the world and the souls of its citizens, but he also fought to keep his own authority, and head, on his shoulders. And he hoped, perhaps beyond all sense, that young Catherine did as well.

He swallowed his fear, his anger, and said, "If Catherine fails... she will be executed."

Part One

The Spanish Road

I

Catherine could not take Adaliz's sobbing. It wasn't that she couldn't understand how the little girl felt, for she, in her own way, felt the same. Both of them had lost their fathers: Adaliz's to the Cross of Saint Boniface; Catherine's to his royal obligation. But Catherine had had plenty of time to come to terms with her loss. Poor Adaliz was just finding out about her father. Her brother, Albrecht, was faring better, though his chin was quivering. Being the man of the house now, he had to show strength, regardless of his true feelings (a duty no doubt taught to him by his father). Strength for his sister and for his mother, Rosa. She, on the other hand, was holding nothing back.

"He ordered you to deliver this message to us?"

Catherine winced at the fire, the anger, in Rosa's eyes. She admired it. Here stood a strong, confident woman, one who undoubtedly had stood toe to toe against her very tall and powerful husband and was not above giving her opinion. That, plus the fact that Catherine was not dressed in the finery that would mark her as a daughter of King Ferdinand and Queen Isabella of Spain. She was dressed as she always was these days: more like a man than a woman, dressed down to fit her career as assassin and specialist for the Hanseatic League. What business was it of hers to give Rosa the bad news?

Catherine nodded. "He asked that we share this news with you and your children."

"Share?" Rosa huffed and threw her arms up. "That's a mild way to tell me that my children's father is gone forever."

Catherine winced again. Her companion, Fymurip Azat, chimed in, saving her from another uncomfortable response. "My lady," he said, trying to put his best foot forward. "I dare not assume that my limited association with Lux von Junker is in any way comparable to your love and devotion to him all the years that you have been married. But I can assure you, with complete honesty, that your husband made this decision out of love for you and your children. The Eldar gods will seek the cross, no matter where, or how, it manifests itself. If he had returned here, your lives would have been in danger. Your children -"

"Enough!" Rosa said with a wave of her hand, rising up and walking to a hearth that crackled with burning wood. The wood had a sweet smell that Catherine liked. It helped make the situation bearable.

There was a long pause as Adaliz ran to her mother and hugged her waist. Albrecht just sat there, silent, staring at Fymurip as if he had never seen a Muslim. But of course, that was not true. According to Fymurip, they had met once before in this very city. But the little boy's stare was unnerving, and Catherine could see Fymurip fidget in the seat.

"Thank you both for bringing this information to me and my children," Rosa said, clutching Adaliz to her waist and rubbing the little girl's back. "You may go now."

"My lady, I—"

"Go!"

There was nothing further to be said that would be listened to. Catherine nodded, stood, bowed respectfully to them all, and headed for the door. Fymurip did the same, and they were out quickly and walking through the foggy Avignon streets.

"That went well," Fymurip said. "Better than expected."

Catherine turned to him and blanched. "Went well? That woman had daggers for us, Fymurip. If she had had one, we'd be clutching our severed throats right now."

"Rosa understands the danger of the Eldar gods. She survived them, if what Lux said was true. They faced them in Strasbourg a year ago, before I met up with him. She may not like it, but in her heart, she understands what her husband has done. What he needed to do."

Catherine shrugged. She wasn't so sure. The one thing she knew that men often got wrong about women was the assumption that they needed protecting. Everyone needed protecting from time to time, both men and women. But she was sure that Rosa would have preferred that she and her husband face whatever dangers awaited them together, and Lux should have been more aware of Rosa's strength. Of course, putting children in harm's way changed the nature of the threat. Catherine understood that, so maybe it was best that the Teutonic knight had gone east to Cathay to face his demons alone. Catherine sighed. The situation was such a mess.

"Where do we go now?" Fymurip asked as they reached a crossroad and paused.

Catherine looked both ways, trying to remember where the message boy had told her to meet her contact from the League. Left? No, right. Yes, that was the way.

"This way," she said, and headed out, dodging a cart to avoid being splattered with mud. "We're meeting someone."

Fymurip stepped over a muddy puddle and followed. "Who?"

*****

Fymurip saw the League member the minute they stepped through the door. Amidst the clamber and riotous laughter and rowdiness of the tavern patrons, the man was easy to spot. He wore newly pressed clothing, a fur-trimmed blue over-gown with split hanging sleeves over a jerkin and embroidered black doublet. A deep blue bonnet covered his curly black hair. On his face lay a well-coifed black goatee. Fymurip shook his head. The man was definitely overgroomed and overdressed for the occasion, but then, that didn't surprise him. A deep arrogance and self-importance flowed through the veins of most members of the Hanseatic League. He had seen such arrogance on display in Lübeck not more than a year ago. Had almost wasted away in prison because of it. Catherine had saved him.

Fymurip looked at Catherine and saw the stark difference between her and the League's man. She wore plain black-and-tan pantaloons and a long-sleeved shirt with an attached hood. Utilitarian. Simple. Fymurip smiled. He'd take Catherine's kind of presentation over anyone else's at any time.

When the man saw them, he stood, snapped his fingers, and two additional chairs were produced by the tavern staff. And wine. Fymurip waved it off, though the smell was appetizing. Catherine took a small portion in a brass cup. Then they all settled around a round table.

"Welcome to Avignon," the man said. "My name is Adamo Rosini."

"Italian, eh?" Fymurip flashed a smirk. "You are far from home."

"As are you, Muslim."

There was an insult in Rosini's words, a racial and religious animosity, and Fymurip considered reaching for the Kurdish khanjar dagger which he had tucked into his boot. He let it go. Perhaps he had insulted the man by reminding him that he was Italian. Some did not like being reminded either.

"You have word from the League?" Catherine asked.

Rosini nodded. He leaned forward and lowered his voice. "Yes, I do. Straight from Georg himself, and not to be ignored or refused." Rosini cleared his throat, reached into his doublet's pocket, and pulled out a folded note. He handed it to Catherine. "The words on that bit of parchment are paramount, Catherine, and you must remind yourself of them as you make your way to Spain. But I am also ordered to give you Georg's order verbally, and it is thus: you are to go to Marcilla Castle in Navarre, find the sword Tizona, take it, and deliver it to Georg yourself. You Catherine, not anyone else. Certainly not an ex-Tatar soldier whose arrogance eclipses only my own."

Again, Fymurip considered reaching for his dagger. He stared deep into Rosini's face. The man was not as effete as he first seemed under all those layers of wealthy, refined cloth. The brash Italian knew himself well, knew how he must look amidst all these French low-life drunkards. He was certainly arrogant. But he wasn't afraid, and Fymurip admired that.

Catherine's face turned pale as she stared at the words in the note. Fymurip leaned back to try to see the words. Catherine folded up the parchment quickly and tucked it into her boot. "Very well," she said, taking a sip of wine from her cup. Fymurip could see her handshake as she drank. She finished and then cleared her throat. "I need more men. I cannot do this with only one companion."

"You must," Rosini said, his face showing sincerity. "A larger force would draw unwarranted attention, and you know this. Spain is your country, Catherine, your home. There are other League members there, yes, but this is your mission. After all, it was your father who gave the sword to Ezpeleta as a gift."

Fymurip waved his hand. "Wait, I'm not familiar with this sword you speak of. And who is Ezpeleta?"

Rosini chuckled, finished his wine, put the cup down, and rose from his chair. He straightened himself, fixed his clothing, and put a hand on Fymurip's shoulder. "Catherine will fill you in on everything you need to know. And take care, my friend. The Spanish aren't very fond of Muslims these days, especially the king and queen."

Rosini nodded respectfully to Catherine, said, "Good luck, my lady," and then walked out.

Fymurip sat there staring at Catherine, who was still as pale as a ghost. Something was wrong. Something was contained in the note that Rosini had handed her that far exceeded his words of warning about Spain. "What is the matter?"

Catherine turned to him. She tried to smile, and then her face grew a light shade of green. She covered her mouth, burped, and said, "I'm going to be sick."

II

Fymurip held Catherine's hair back in a ponytail, to ensure that it was not spattered with her vomit. She was hunched over outside the tavern, heaving the contents of her stomach into the street. Patrons leaving the tavern took a wide berth. Some smiled and pointed; others laughed. Fymurip might have joined in with them, if the situation weren't so dire.

"This is why I do not drink," he said to her, as he dared to place his hand on her shoulder for comfort. "That wine was strong. I could smell it—"

"It wasn't the wine," she said, interrupting. She coughed, wiped her mouth, and stood up slowly. Fymurip let her hair go. Her color was returning. "It's this damned mission. It's the thought of having to return to Spain, to Navarre, to get Tizona."

"What is Tizona?" He asked. "I do not know anything about it."

Catherine collected herself further and stretched her back as she walked a few paces away from Fymurip and found a spot against the tavern wall on which to lean. She rubbed her face, sighed, and said, "Tizona was a sword once owned by El Cid. You do know who he was, correct?"

Of course, he did. Everyone in the Muslim faith knew of El Cid, whether they were Moorish or had travelled to Spain or not.

His true name was Rodrigo Díaz de Vivar, more commonly known as "El Cid," meaning 'The Lord' in Arabic. He was a Castilian nobleman and military leader who had lived over 500 years ago. Christians referred to him as El Campeador which, if Fymurip's Spanish was correct, meant 'Outstanding Warrior'. He was indeed that, as he fought for both Christians and Muslims during his lifetime. He was a legend in both the collective minds of Europe and the Middle East. He was loved and despised on both sides of the religious divide. Fymurip remembered, as a child, listening to stories of El Cid's battlefield prowess.

"Yes, I know of him," Fymurip said. "He named his sword. Many warriors do. What is the issue?"

"Tizona is no normal sword, Fymurip," Catherine said, shaking her head, "and the League doesn't want it for its metallurgy or its value in gold. It's magical."

Fymurip nodded, still confused. "Before we left Starybogow, you stated that the League was seeking a sword, and you suggested clearly that the Eldar gods were seeking it as well. So, we were aware of why we were heading to Spain. Again: what is the problem?"

Catherine coughed, stood straight. "There are thousands of swords in the world, Fymurip. Hundreds of those have some magical properties in one way or another. I had no idea that Tizona was the sword they sought."

Now Fymurip was growing annoyed. Catherine was dancing around the issue, answering his questions, but not truly wanting to divulge all the information that he needed to understand the situation. "Come," he said, holding out his hand to offer support. "Let's return to our room and discuss this privately."

He wasn't sure if she was going to agree, but finally she nodded and took his hand.

They walked three blocks to another tavern that had a few small rooms for rent. They had acquired one the night before. It was so small and the bed so narrow that Fymurip had to find comfort leaned up in a corner. He had spent all night listening to Catherine snore, falling in and out of fitful sleep himself. Having to play a cat-and-mouse game with her now to get the information he needed was not his idea of the best way to start a mission.

"Now," he said, as they settled into their room. "Tell me about this Tizona. Everything you know."

It looked as if she were going to obfuscate again, then Catherine settled down on her bed, leaned back, folded her arms, and began to speak. "Tizona means 'firebrand', and some say that it is simply a term used to denote any sword of noteworthiness. There have been other weapons, like lances for instance, called Tizon or Tizona, what have you. So, its name isn't really the issue or the reason for my concern. My concern is that this sword was once wielded by El Cid, and that undoubtedly makes it one of the most powerful swords in the world."

"What is its magic?" Fymurip asked.

Catherine shook her head. "I do not know. Like a lot of artifacts in this world that contain magical properties, its true nature comes to light only when the right person, under the right conditions, wields it. In that sense, it is a lot like The Cross of Saint Boniface. But a cross is a cross, and by its very shape and nature, is not an object of war. A sword is an object of war, Fymurip. You know this better than anyone. Therefore, its magic would be very, very powerful in the right — or wrong — hands."

Fymurip nodded. "That's probably why the League seeks it: to ensure that it doesn't fall into those hands."

"Yes," Catherine agreed, "but... there's more." She fidgeted on the bed like a young girl might, trying to get the best comfort for her back and backside. When she was finished, she continued. "After El Cid's death, Tizona, like many artifacts, passed from hand to hand, and eventually fell into my father's keeping. He, in turn, gifted it to Pedro de Peralta y Ezpeleta, the first Count of Santisteban of Lerín, for his dedicated service in the negotiation of the marriage agreement between my father and my mother. Giving Tizona away was very difficult for my father, for El Cid had brought great misery to Aragon in his service to the Moors. Possessing that sword gave my family pride and a strong sense of revenge. So, for my father to give it as a gift to anyone was difficult. For me, his daughter, to go to Navarre, to Marcilla Castle, and take it back... well, that would constitute treason in the eyes of my father. In his heart, he may indeed long to have it back, but the political ramifications of having his own flesh and blood reacquire it through theft would be too difficult to bear."

Catherine paused, and Fymurip did not speak, waiting to see if she would continue. "I have not known you for very long, Catherine," he said after a time. "A year, perhaps? But in that time, I've never gotten the impression that you were overly concerned with bringing shame or dishonor to your family name. I mean no disrespect when I say that. What I mean is that, being in service to the Hanseatic League, doing the things that you do for them, I can't imagine that stealing a sword from a castle could be any worse than what you have already done."

Fymurip grimaced to himself. His words had not come out right. He was trying to pay her a compliment, trying to point out her incredibly independent spirit and skills that few men even possessed. Surely the fact that she had left home, all but denying her royalty and family name by doing so, had left her father, mother, and family angry beyond calculation. How could a simple heist make things any worse?

He tried once again. Catherine cut him off with a wave. "You don't have to say anything more, Fymurip. I know what you're trying to say. And yes, you are right. I have done many things that could easily force my father to disown me and cast me aside, and being a girl makes it all the more painful for him. It is one thing to work in the shadows in Germany, East Prussia, Starybogow, and wherever else, far, far away from home. But Spain is my home, and they are my people. My father is Aragonese; my mother Castellan. If I break into Marcilla Castle and steal a sword that my father had given a nobleman for his service, that would be seen as an insult beyond words, and might spur a rebellion, a civil war. Spain is unified once again under one banner. My mother and father's marriage is the reason for that. Do I dare risk breaking that unification?"

It was a valid question, Fymurip had to admit, but perhaps too late in the game to consider? Meeting with Rosini, hearing him give Georg's orders, and not objecting, was acceptance of the mission. Catherine could indeed, if she chose, ignore the order, return to her father, and become that which she was born to be: a princess for sure, a queen perhaps. But Fymurip doubted that that was where this conversation was headed.

"Besides," Catherine said, "my father will most certainly learn of Tizona's theft, and he will come seeking the thief."

"You are more than capable of staying out of harm's way," Fymurip said.

"And," she continued, ignoring his subtle compliment, "he will insist that I marry that wretched boy, Arthur Tudor, Prince of Wales." She paused as if she were going to throw up again, then shook her head and continued. "I'm betrothed to him."

There was the reason Fymurip was looking for, the real reason. That excuse he could accept as her concern about the mission. In the year that he had known her, had travelled with her, he knew one immutable truth about the girl: Catherine of Aragon was nobody's breed whore.

What does she think of me? He wondered. She had kissed him on the cheek a few times, hugged him a couple, but all of those gestures seemed innocent, like simple acknowledgments for good service or deeds. And he had never tried to pursue such shows of affection with any form of aggressive action or affection of his own. But he did wonder sometimes, and sometimes... Fymurip shook his head and put those amorous thoughts out of his mind. Now was not the time for such distractions.

"I'll steal it," he said, blurting out the words before he gave them much thought. "You deliver me to Marcilla Castle, and I'll go in and get it."

"Ha!" Catherine's voice lilted up as if she were singing a hymn. "You're good, Fymurip, but not that good. That castle's a fortress."

Fymurip snickered, shook his head. "How quickly we forget. I survived years in the pits as a fighter, survived an attack from a Vucari, survived years of struggle in Starybogow. I survived an Eldar God intent on eating me alive, do you not remember? I think I can handle the stone ramparts of a castle, no matter how thick or high they are."

He could see that Catherine was about to say something sarcastic, but she stilled, wiggled her nose to keep from sneezing, rubbed her face, then said, "Very well, but that will not keep me out of Spain."

Fymurip shrugged. "Sorry... that I cannot help you with. But if it's me who takes the sword, a Tatar, a Muslim, a Saracen, that is to be expected. The crime will not befall you, even if, in the end, you personally deliver it to Georg. His message to you was for you to deliver the sword in person, but you do not have to be the one to pluck it from its current resting place."

She nodded. She closed her eyes, and for a moment, he thought she had fallen asleep. Then she opened them, yawned, and said, "Very well. Thank you. When do we go?"

"In the morning, after breakfast and prayers."

Catherine nodded then blew out the candle on the small wooden stand next to her bed. "Goodnight, Fymurip. Rest fast."

He rested as fast as he could, and he was nearly asleep when he remembered that he had forgotten to ask her about the note from Georg that she had stuffed into her boot.

But she was already asleep and snoring.

III

Pamplona was a Spanish city in Navarre that had seen its share of turmoil. From its very beginnings during the Roman conquest, to the more recent struggle between the Beaumont and Agramont confederacies, it had changed hands several times. So much so that, for centuries, it was treated more like a fortress than a city, reinforcing its walls over and over to await and then (hopefully) repulse the next foreign invader. Even Catherine's own father had taken it by force when he had come to power. Now, under the combined rule of her mother and father, Navarre once again functioned like its own independent state. So long as it paid fealty to the crown and served her family both in times of war and peace, Pamplona was left alone. But peace, especially in Spain, was always fickle, and anything, like stealing an ancient sword, could break that peace.

Now here Catherine stood, in the quiet of a room above a Pamplona tavern, with a sketch of the Castillo de Marcilla scribbled hastily on a stretched piece of tan bull hide, wondering why she had ever agreed to let Fymurip fight her battles. Knowing full well what Georg's note meant—which was still tucked into her boot and probably wet and smelly from sweat and road dust—how could she possibly allow him to assault this mighty fortress on his own when so much was at stake? The only positive thought she could muster was that Marcilla Castle, by normal castle standards, was relatively small and box shaped.

She pointed at the castle's courtyard. "The central court takes up a lot of internal space. That is good. It means that you will not have to contend with a long, tedious exploration. You can start searching at one corner and work your way around."

Fymurip nodded. "It's not as large as the Yeni Saray in Istanbul, Allah be praised. The walls are still thick, however, which means that there are a lot of rooms and passages to navigate. Do you have an idea of where the sword lays?"

Catherine shook her head. "The man who sold me this sketch was not entirely sure, but he thinks here." She pointed to a portion of the castle just off the courtyard. "This is the throne room. It's an internal room, so you will have to move through whatever security they have no matter where you scale the wall. That concerns me, for we are not too far from the Reconquista, which means that Moorish traps may still be in place."

Fymurip seemed confused, shook his head. "But the Moors controlled only portions of Navarre, and not for very long before you Christians began to throw them back. How can their traps still be in place?"

Catherine held in her mirth. "When you're dealing with supernatural forces, Fymurip, a thousand years is a day. If the League taught me anything, it is that that power of the gods is eternal."

Fymurip rolled his eyes and sighed. "Why are we always in the midst of such supernatural forces? And why do we never employ our own forces in support?"

That was not always true, as the events in and around Starybogow had proven, and Catherine knew that Fymurip was aware of such things. He was just being grumpy. He was tired, hungry, and probably having second thoughts about offering to steal the sword without her aid. But they were here in Navarre, in Pamplona, and just a couple days ride from Marcilla. There was no turning back now.

Fymurip pointed to the northeastern corner of the castle. "I think I should scale the wall here. It's a little further away from the throne room, but it's also the furthest corner from the main battlement. Eyes will be upon me quickly, so a night assault would be best. We need to find me some dark clothes like those you wore in Lübeck."

"Very well." Catherine rolled up the sketch and put it aside. "Let's go buy you a wardrobe."

*****

They worked the streets of Pamplona. There was a gentle rain, and so it was easy for Fymurip to pull up the hood of his cloak and go unnoticed and unimpeded through the streets. Passers-by looked at them, of course, as people tend to do, but they were not harassed in any way. Fymurip had tucked his khanjar dagger into his belt just in case.

"My blades are growing dull," he said to Catherine as they walked towards a clothier with its door wide open. "They need a whetstone."

"You'll have ample opportunity for that as we head to Mar-cilla," Catherine said. "It's two days ride south. You can use mine, though I know swordsmen prefer their own stone. After finding your clothes, we'll hunt for one. Perhaps we can find a blacksmith with a Belgian bluestone. They're the best."

Fymurip nodded. Normally, he carried his own, as Catherine had alluded to, but the past several months had been hectic as they had made their way from Starybogow. He woke up one morning, and his stone was gone, lost somewhere, he supposed, along the road. His Turkish kilij sword needed a sharpening badly, for it was showing real wear, especially at the tip. His khanjar dagger could barely cut butter.

He was about to laugh at his own joke when Catherine sud-denly stopped before entering the clothier's entrance, put her arm out to stop his movement, and stared down the cobbled street to-wards a line of bulls. "Can you see them?" she asked.

"Yes." But what was he looking at precisely, was the ques-tion on his mind? For these bulls were not the kind that one might encounter at a bullfight somewhere in Spain, or the kind that Pam-plona was famous for. No. These were ethereal bulls, white and grey and thin as smoke. There were four of them, spread out shoulder to shoulder across the street, barring the passage. They held the shape of bulls, but not the actual flesh and blood. They were smooth, their musculature undefined, as if they had been, in life, carved from granite. They snorted and dug at the street with hooves worn from centuries of rain and wind. The rain passed through them like light fog.

Catherine pulled a knife from her belt. "Come with me." Fymurip pulled his dagger and followed her into the street. "What are you doing?"

Catherine paused to bend her knees and fix herself into a de-fensive stance. She held her knife forward, leveling the sharp tip to-wards the eyes of the central bull. "I'm facing them."

Fymurip swallowed his apprehension. The last time he had faced ethereal creatures like these, he was in Istanbul, watching a Jinn and an Efreet tear each other apart over the body of a dead mys-tic. What could small handheld blades do to four powerful bulls?

"Follow my movements."

He tried matching her movements. He held his dagger forward like she was doing, switching it from hand to hand, but always keeping it leveled against the bulls. She shifted her weight from left to right leg, then back again, taunting the bulls, showing no fear. For their part, they stood there, stone-like, watching, waiting. Waiting for what? Fymurip did not know, but when Catherine moved, he moved.

Civilians who had been walking the street were now taking a wide berth, as if they knew what was happening, and Fymurip wondered if they too saw the bulls like he did. They seemed to, as their speech now mimicked Catherine's. Fymurip's Spanish was adequate, but not functional in any way. He did not understand the words Catherine's was speaking, for he did not understand the context, and so much about understanding someone else's language was about context. But he mouthed the words anyway, giving support to her movements. He felt silly, here in the rain, mouthing unusual Spanish words and dancing like he was drunk.

Then Catherine stopped, and screamed, Carguen! He knew exactly what that meant.

Charge!

The bulls obliged, moving together. First, very slowly, but within five paces, they had moved from a trot to a full-bodied sprint. They charged quietly, their powerful, smoky legs making no sound as they trundled forward. Fymurip would have preferred to hear their hooves pounding the cobbles. Their silent movement was terrifying, and his hand trembled as he held his dagger forward. He closed his eyes and waited.

The bulls hit, and despite their corporeal bodies, he was tossed into the air as the horns of one of the bulls caught him in the chest and tossed him up. The horns seemed to pierce his skin, but he felt no pain. Catherine was tossed up as well, but in her descent, she slashed at the bulls with her blade, cutting huge swaths through their backs. The cuts looked strong, lethal, but they were bloodless and closed quickly. Fymurip did the same. His cuts were equally strong, but the bulls moved right through them, oblivious to any damage.

Fymurip hit the street hard. He grimaced as he fought against pain in his chest as his ribs fought against breaking. They had been broken many times before, and he had no desire to see them broken again. He quickly supported his weight with his arms, turned his head, and watched as the bulls charged down the street and past the clothier. Then they shot into the sky and disappeared in gentle wisps of smoke.

They were gone, and the citizens in witness began to cheer. Fymurip huffed and pushed himself up slowly into a sitting position. He did not share in their excitement.

"You handled that well," Catherine said, helping him to his feet. "Very commendable."

"What were they?"

"Those, my friend, were spirit bulls from Guisando. They protect Avila Spain from harm." Catherine wrinkled her brow, bit her lip. "They are far from home. That is worrisome."

"Why were they here?" Fymurip asked.

"They serve as a warning: tread lightly or be trampled to death. They can appear to anyone who has come to Spain with evil intent. Seeing them here, so far from home, means only one thing."

"What?"

Catherine's excitement of his handling of the bulls was gone. Her face grew long, serious. "They know we are here."

IV

Who "they" were was difficult for Catherine to define. Maybe her father. Maybe Eldar cultists. Maybe a third party with knowledge of their mission and who were thus intent on thwarting the effort. Maybe the Inquisition. Fymurip didn't like moving forward with the knowledge that there was someone out there keeping an eye on their travels by sending supernatural creatures to give them a warning. That kind of sorcery was most troubling. "You're lucky it was just a warning," Catherine said as they saddled up their horses the next morning. "If they had sent the real Guisando bulls, we'd be dead."

Apparently, the real bulls were made of pure granite, were centuries old, and each weighed over a thousand pounds. In all of his travels, Fymurip was content in the knowledge that he had never fought against animated rock. The thought of finally facing such creatures was most troubling indeed.

They set out anyway, Catherine in the lead. The trip from Pamplona to Marcilla castle would take two days nominally, and hopefully fair weather would help hasten them along. It rained a portion of the first day, and so they were forced to stop early and head out at first light the next. The delay was stressful, for Fymurip wanted to get into the action, to stop thinking about it, worrying about what might or might not occur behind those thick castle walls. The slower pace, however, did allow him to sharpen his blades. They had not been successful in finding him a Belgian Bluestone, but a blacksmith had been willing to part with his personal stone for a modest fee. It took a little while for Fymurip to get used to it. It sat differently in his hand than the one he had carried, and it had a different grain of coarseness. But it worked, and both dagger and sword were now clean, shiny, and as sharp as razors.

They arrived at dusk on the second day, making sure to leave their horses at a livery on the edge of the town of Marcilla itself. The map that they had reviewed about the complex did not, unfortunately, tell the entire story. The castle itself, though small, sat in the midst of many common houses and businesses.

"Curse our bad fortune," Fymurip hissed, as he quickly donned the black shirt and breeches that they had found in Pamplona. Then he wrapped his forehead with a black scarf. "The blasted thing couldn't be isolated in the woods or on a mountainside? It had to be in the middle of a town."

"That's a good thing, isn't it?" Catherine asked. "There's more cover and more shadow. We can disappear into those dark streets before they see us."

Fymurip shook his head. "Having civilians around means more fingers pointing in the direction of our retreat. If this were Starybogow, I'd rejoice. The ruins of that cursed place hold its secrets well. Marcilla is no Starybogow. A mob can form quickly here, and then we'll be cutting our way through innocents."

Catherine had a troubled look, and Fymurip thought that perhaps his gloomy disposition, which had possessed him the last couple days, was beginning to weigh on her conscience. "My apologies, Catherine. I do not mean to despair. I have agreed to undertake this mission, and I will do so. It is for a good cause, I know. I just wish the odds were, at least once, in our favor. And I wish I were on more familiar ground. Spain is lovely, but it is not my home."

"Neither was Prussia," Catherine said, "but you managed well there."

"Years traipsing through those dark, wooded lands can give a man the right confidence. This place is new to me."

She nodded but said nothing more.

Catherine helped him check his sword and dagger to ensure that they were well buckled at his waist. She checked the cloth around his head to ensure the knot was tight and would not slip. Then she handed him his rope and grapple hook and helped him secure it on his shoulder. Everything was in place. It was time to go.

"Wish me luck," Fymurip said as he nodded, smiled, and turned to go.

"You're Muslim," Catherine said. "You don't believe in luck."

Fymurip chuckled, paused, turned, and said, "You're right. I told you that you Christians would be the death of me."

*****

He reached the northeastern corner of the castle with a careful application of guile and stealth. There were guards patrolling the outside perimeter of the walls, down inside the ditch encircling the castle. There was no water in that ditch, Allah be praised, but it did offer its own challenges. Going down into that ditch and then trying to toss the grapple straight up the high wall would be difficult at best, and studying the timing of the guards as they patrolled meant that he had only three, perhaps four, tosses before a guard would turn the corner and see him, no matter how dark his clothing. Sconces placed twenty feet apart at eye level, with fresh torches burning brightly, gave off more light than Fymurip desired. He sighed. *We can never catch a break.*

He'd have to do this another way.

Standing on the lip of the ditch put him roughly five extra feet higher in relation to the wall than if he were down there with the guards. That was good, for it meant that his angle for tossing the grapple would be better. But did he have the arm strength to do it? If Lux were here, he'd get the old brute to show off his strength. The Teutonic knight could toss the hook like a pebble across a lake. Fymurip wished that he were inclined to use crossbows. He wished he had one, for he'd seen people in Starybogow use them to launch grapples up walls.

He hefted the grapple in his left hand, letting the attached rope coil on the ground. Catherine had purchased wisely: the tool had a good weight, it was well-balanced, and finely crafted. It would hold on to the parapet for sure. He just needed to toss it up there.

He waited quietly in the dark until the guard closest to him turned the corner. Fymurip stepped back five paces, letting the grapple drop to just a few inches from the ground. He held the rope tightly, drew back his arm, and began to twirl the rope and hook. Slowly at first, to ensure that he got a good twist on it. He twirled it like he'd seen slingers twirl their leather projectile pouch, going faster and faster as the rhythm of the twirl grew consistent and pronounced. He could feel the wind off the rope.

Then he let go so that the hook flew freely through the air, up and at a slight angle, towards the parapet of the castle. Before throwing, he calculated that he was roughly forty feet away. Catherine had given him sixty feet of rope, more than enough to scale the wall.

The hook struck the parapet and fell to the ground.

Fymurip cursed silently, gnashed his teeth, and pulled the hook back.

He tossed again, adding even more turns, more muscle. His arm was beginning to ache, but it fell short again.

On the third try, he backed up a few additional paces, began to twirl, and when the hook was at its fastest rotation, he ran forward five steps—as he had seen slingers do it—and then let fly. That extra impetus did the trick: the hook flew over the parapet with a few feet to spare.

He pulled back and hooked the grapple. He tugged it several times to ensure its strength. Then he reached up the rope, held it tightly, and launched.

The Tartar flew through the air. His boots struck the wall about six feet above the ditch. His right knee cracked on impact, and he held in a scream. There was pain, but it didn't feel like anything had been broken or torn. That was a relief, and some good luck. He wanted to rest a moment to let his body recover from the impact, but he could hear the loud, armored gait of a guard coming his way. Fymurip took three strong breaths, then began to climb.

It was a relatively easy climb, despite the pain in his knee. The castle wall was rough, and his soft leather boots held against it well. He pulled himself up, hand over hand, until he was able to grab the parapet and pull himself over the top.

He crouched on the rampart walkway, paused, and took a look around. There were guards pacing the walls here as well, but fewer, and his luck held. The closest was still many feet away. So Fymurip unhooked the grapple and pulled up the rope quickly to ensure that those patrolling below did not find it. Where he would stow the grapple in the castle, he did not know. He was not about to sneak around with a heavy rope and hook hanging from his shoulder, but he'd find a place for it before proceeding too far. There was always some corner in a castle, out of easy sight, for hiding such things.

Like the ditch below, there was ample torch light along the ramparts. Fymurip was glad for this illumination, for using it would ensure easier visibility when he decided where he was going to descend into the courtyard. Catherine had recommended against exposing himself by entering the yard but looking now at the internal layout of the building—what parts he could actually see and ascertain in the shadows—suggested that the only safe way down was over the inner wall. There were two sets of staircases on either end of the castle which allowed for movement up and down from the inner structures of the palace, but they were being guarded by two men each. Fymurip was certain he could make short work of them all, but he'd prefer not to bloody his blades until absolutely necessary. They were thirsty, indeed, but it would be more prudent to try to find Tizona without shedding much blood.

He looked down into the courtyard. About a twenty-foot drop. Manageable, though he'd have to be cautious about impact. He could scarcely afford breaking a knee or compressing his spine. A hit and roll maneuver. He'd done them before.

Fymurip crouched and waited another moment to ensure none of the guards were near enough to see him drop. Then, using his right hand for balance, he leapt.

He struck soft ground in the courtyard and rolled. The rope and grapple on his shoulder caused an imbalance, so his recovery was less than stellar. He slid a little as his left shoulder struck dirt. Some pain, but manageable.

Luckily, there were a few green bushes interspersed in flowerbeds that provided good hiding places for his grapple. Fymurip collected himself, and then tucked the grapple away under one of the bushes. He then drew his dagger and stood up. He turned, and there stood a man, staring back at him.

The man was clearly a servant. His clothes were delicate, of fine white fabric, and in no way provided protection from blades. He held a glass goblet in one hand and a pitcher of wine in the other. Fymurip could smell the sweet fermented berries.

The man tried to shout. Fymurip drew his blade across the man's throat before he uttered a word.

Fymurip caught the man before he fell. He let the goblet and wine slip to the ground. The wine splashed, but neither object broke nor alerted the guards. He pulled the dying man to the bushes and laid him down gently, covering him as best he could with leaves, grass, and branches.

But such cover would not last for long, he knew. Whoever had ordered the wine would come looking, and they'd find this poor, innocent man soon enough, who just happened to be in the wrong place at the wrong time.

Fymurip wiped his dagger across the grass to clean it, took a deep breath, and headed towards a well-lit colonnade. He cursed to himself.

Why can't I catch a break?

V

Catherine hated waiting, but the plan was for Fymurip to go in by himself, find, and steal the sword, thus freeing her of any direct involvement. But it was too dangerous, too risky for him to go in alone. Why had she agreed to it? Was she so afraid that the Ezpeleta family would implicate her father—and by extension, the Crown—of the theft, that she was willing to sacrifice a friend that had, on more than one occasion, saved her life over the past year? Was she that cowardly? And was Fymurip just a friend, or more? She did not know the answer to that last question. She thought that her feelings for him were clear after the Eldar God incident in Starybogow. But as they had travelled back to France and now into Spain, her feelings had become muddled, unclear, the weight of her responsibility as a princess of the Crown, a daughter to the king and queen, had begun to cloud her judgement, confuse her feelings. Did she love Fymurip? She wasn't sure, but if, in the end, she did, then why in God's name did she let him go in there alone?

She moved around the castle, far enough away so that she could take advantage of cover and shadow on the perimeter of the Marcilla township. The castle was a rare structure in Spain in that it marked the absolute center of the town, and it lacked the stunning opulence of other castles, like her father's. The Marcilla citizens could wake up every morning, peer out their doors, and see their castle standing tall and secure in the middle of their town. It must be a comforting feeling, Catherine thought, as she slowly made her way around the castle until she could see the open drawbridge. And I'm about to violate that comfort.

The drawbridge was open, and men huddled around a small wagon whose driver begged admittance into the castle. It was taking some time to approve the shipment of barrels and crates and sacks that lay in a heap in the back of the wagon. Catherine studied the pile as best as she could from her vantage point. She shook her head and winced. There did not appear to be hiding room for a body amongst those goods, even a body as slender as hers. Beneath the wagon, however, was another matter. It was a low-sitting wagon, but again, she was slender, and could easily wiggle her way underneath.

The wagon sat half on and half off the bridge. The low wall at the end of the bridge did offer some cover and was about five feet from the wagon, if she could just get there unseen. From there, her situation would improve immensely.

Fymurip wore the darkest clothing, but hers wasn't overly bright either. Earth tones, tan and brown, dark boots. She was well-dressed for night work, and it had been awhile since she had had need to do any stealth activity. She was excited, and she let that excitement get the better of her.

She stood and simply walked out into the small path that ran along the lip of the castle's ditch. It was a footpath more than anything, but there were some civilians making their way along that path, and Catherine just walked out in the midst of them, not even bothering to cover her sword which hung from her belt. The people drew back from her, afraid. She hesitated, considered jumping back into cover to reassess, then she had an idea.

Muevense, she said in full Spanish, drawing her sword. It had been awhile since she had been able to speak her native language. Fymruip knew some of it but not enough for fluent speaking. It felt good. El castillo esta ocupado esta noche. Muevense.

It wasn't so much what she said, but how she said it: with a note of authority that people naturally deferred to. Whether they truly believed that she, a girl, was part of the castle guard or no, didn't really matter. She just needed them to be confused long enough to move quickly out of the way so that she could return to the task at hand, and before the wagon moved inside. They could decide her validity later on around their respective dinner tables.

When the people were gone, Catherine sheathed her sword, crouched down at the top of the ditch, and moved quietly into place.

The castle guards around the wagon were arguing with the driver about the late delivery. The driver was trying to explain that he had been held up outside of town by corrupt merchants who were trying to charge him too much, knowing that his wares were heading to the castle. The shipment should have been here hours ago, one guard said. And it went on like that for a while, with the guards having the arrogance to suggest that the driver pay them a *honorarios pequenos* (a small fee) for entrance at such a late hour. But the driver was stubborn and would not budge, arguing back that if the Ezpeletas did not get the goods that they had already paid for, there'd be tough questions to answer later. Catherine smiled. She admired the driver's pluck in the presence of so many armed guards, but she had a notion that perhaps he had endured this kind of treatment in the past, and it was all part of the game.

In the end, he tossed them a couple coins. The guards were satisfied with that and let him pass.

She waited until the guards had walked back across the drawbridge. When the wagon began to roll, she followed.

First, right behind the wagon. It moved slowly, and that was good, for it gave her time to catch up and then crawl crab-like until she was lying beneath the undercarriage of the wagon. Then she flipped over, as fast as her body could move, before the wagon pressed on and left her exposed on the bridge. She flipped and reached up for the sway bar and reach socket, grabbed them tightly, and pulled herself up. She wrapped her left leg around the hound brace so that her right leg could dangle there, an inch off the ground, and keep her sword from scraping the bridge. It was a painful, difficult position to be in, and Catherine held her breath against muscles that had gone a bit soft over the past couple months. Now she wanted the driver to whip his horses, to get them moving, so she did not have to endure this pain much longer.

But she was flush against the bottom of the wagon, and thus her exposure was minimal. She was in a good place, so long as the wagon kept a steady pace and did not jerk or strike a rock or anything else, she'd be fine.

The wagon halted just inside the castle, and another round of discussions and inspections of the goods occurred. This time it was someone from the kitchen, a woman's voice. She scolded the driver for being late, but did not expect coinage like the guards had, nor did she linger and waste time. She accepted the goods on review, then ordered her boys to begin unloading. Catherine had to wait a little longer, holding herself against screaming muscles, until the boys removed part of the load, and then walked away for a moment. The driver had drifted off as well on an invite from the lady who offered him a plate of food. The guards too had left. She was alone.

She let herself down slowly and lay there a moment to recover her strength. Her arms and legs were weak, but she didn't have a lot of time to rest. The boys would be back for more crates, and worse, the guards might return.

Catherine rolled out from beneath the wagon, collected herself, and then stood. She drew her sword. A quick glance around the foyer revealed three exits. Which one to take? She wondered. Down one, the light was too bright. Down a second was dark, uninviting. Down the third… well, the smell of cooked meat and bread was delightful, and quite tempting, but no. That way lay the kitchen she was certain, and probably the dining hall. Too many people would be down that exit. And excessive light was not something she worked well in. So down the dark passage she would go. She crouched, shook her head, and slowly made her way into the darkness.

Why am I always walking down dark paths?

*****

Marcilla Castle was well-constructed. Fymurip was impressed. Two levels of living space lay within its walls, accessible through a network of passages and stairways that weren't overly complicated or twisting. Very negotiable, though that itself was a detriment. There weren't many places for a thief like him to hide.

The castle was alive. Lots of activity, and he spent excessive time moving, stopping, waiting for passersby, and then moving a few feet further to do it all over again. The layout of the castle that he had confined to memory told him that he was near the throne room, but he just couldn't get there without major disruption. And now his passage was blocked by three guards, in chain and leather armor. Beyond them lay the throne room, he was certain of it, and he could see no other way there.

Wait! There was a staircase up to the second floor, and though his eyes could be deceiving him, another staircase lay just beyond the guards. Given the uniformity of the castle's construction, the chances of him going up one level, crossing over to the other stairway and back down again, was great. What was up there on the second floor, he wondered, to give him pause? No worse than down here, he figured, though such things were always uncertain. Such concern had never stopped him in the past, Fymurip admitted, and it wouldn't now.

He sneaked up the winding stairs like a dog so that his center was low, strong. He clutched his dagger between his teeth, breathed through his nose. He reached the top of the stairs, paused, took the dagger from his mouth, and stood. He stepped quietly out into the corridor and gazed down towards the second flight of stairs going down. He was right, and luckily, there was no one guarding his passage.

He started out slowly, towards the staircase, dagger in loose fist. He was almost there, then he paused.

A low, threatening growl stopped him.

VI

Her service to the Hanseatic League had given her good instincts in the dark, but her eyes were what they were, and sometimes it took a while for them to adjust. Deeper and deeper into the castle she moved, and the way became darker with each turn. Catherine wasn't sure if the way she was going was the right, most efficient, route. She hadn't studied the map of the castle like Fymurip had; she wasn't supposed to be here, so why bother? But here she was, and certain that the throne room was near. It had to be. Another question before her was more concerning: where was Fymurip?

The intrepid Tatar soldier had to be near. The castle wasn't large enough for them to be separated for long, but things were lively tonight. The castle occupants were active, and there was a sense of calm that gave her surprise, and happily, relief. It did not appear that Fymurip's presence had been discovered. She was grateful for that, but more importantly, she was thankful that her own presence hadn't drawn guards.

Catherine ducked into a small depression in the thick wall which held a pedestal and a very expensive ceramic vase. She accidentally struck the pedestal as she was settling. The vase wobbled, but she managed to catch it before it struck the floor. Lucky for her, for at that very moment, two men walked by, jabbering something in Spanish about the Ezpeleta family and its demand for more Navarre sovereignty. Clearly, the two were in favor of it. Catherine listened in silence, trying to keep her political bias in check. Under her father's rule, Navarre already had reasonable sovereignty, more so than other provinces. She shook her head. Some people were never satisfied with their lot in life.

She waited until they passed, then set the vase back on its pedestal. Slowly, she stepped out into the hallway, let her eyes adjust to the light, and kept moving.

Three more corridors, three more turns, and she was there.

She was surprised that there were no guards in front of the double-wide doors that most certainly led into the throne room. But there was no light emanating from beneath the door, and so it was clear to Catherine that Ezpeleta was not holding court or entertaining guests tonight… at least not on the throne. Guards weren't necessary, really, though, in her experience, it was best to always post a man or two at the entrance of every important room. Ezpeleta had grown overconfident in the comfort and strength of his keep. Who could possibly break in to such a fortress as Marcilla Castle?

She crawled up to the door and tried the latch. Padded and locked. She drew a knife from her belt and worked the blade into the space between the doors. She slid it up to the lock and twisted. The wood was strong, the iron of the lock even stronger. Catherine winced, unhappy. She could bust the lock, but that would take too much time, be too loud, and there was no guarantee that it would work. She sighed and tucked her blade away. There had to be another way into the throne room.

The low, deadly, but muffled growl of a dog echoed through the corridor. Then she heard a man shout.

*****

Fymurip rolled his eyes. He couldn't believe what he saw standing in front of him. Its humped-back shape was ominous and threatening in the faint light, but its red eyes were the most terrifying. It growled like a dog, but Fymurip could see that it was something much, much more.

He thought he had left the wolfman, the Vucari, dead in the bloody ruins of Starybogow, but here it stood. Or, at least, the Spanish equivalent, for this was not the same beast that had haunted him for years in East Prussia. This one seemed taller and lankier, more awkward in its physical presentation. In the shadows, Fymurip could not make out the color of its fur, but it seemed patchier than a Vucari's. Its head was larger, its snout longer. It stood hunched over before him like a man who had been tortured on a stretcher, its arms and legs long with lean muscle. It smelled bad too, like rotten meat, as if it had just feasted on the bloated carcass of a man. And there was no way Fymurip was getting past it.

Fymurip tried to smile. "Good doggy," he said, raising his hand in a gesture of submission. "I have no quarrel with you, my friend. I just need to get past you."

The werewolf did not move. It snapped its maw and growled each time Fymurip moved to the left or right. Every move Fymurip made, the beast matched it, like a mongoose harassing a snake. This wolfman might not be as strong or as savage as the Vucari, but it'd more than make up for those shortcomings with quickness.

I should go back to the first floor, Fymurip thought, glancing behind him to ensure that someone wasn't coming up the staircase to block his retreat. Had he stepped into a trap? Yes, but not an ambush, for there was no one behind him. The only threat lay ahead of him, and it was clear that the castle guards were content to let this creature protect the second floor. That certainly made sense in one way, but foolish in another. No one could control such a beast, not completely anyway. To allow it to roam freely was poor judgement, especially in a castle with women and children. Why had the Ezpeletas employed such a nasty creature as this? Fymurip did not know, but it must be guarding something very, very important. Tizona? Was the sword that valuable, that significant? Perhaps.

No way forward without a fight, and to retreat meant to return to another unsavory situation. And time, as always, was running out.

Fymurip put his dagger in his left hand and pulled his sword with the other. He swiped them both through the air to freshen their edges, then tapped them together to let the werewolf hear their strength and sharpness. The beast seemed unimpressed, unlike those foolish men that he had vanquished again and again in the pit fights. This foe, Fymurip knew, could not be intimidated, at least not with a few fancy moves.

"Very well," Fymurip said, taking a cautious step forward, his blades held in attack posture. "We'll do this the hard way."

Fymurip opened his arms to expose his chest. He barked and growled like a dog, taunting the beast with short jabs of his blades.

The werewolf took the bait. It growled, roared its displeasure, reared back on its long hind legs, then launched.

VII

Fymurip dropped to the floor and let the werewolf fly overhead. He thrust his dagger up and caught the soft underbelly of the beast and drew blood from chest to belly. The werewolf howled in pain, but the cut was not as deep as Fymurip would have liked. The beast had moved so quickly that the slash was nothing more than a glancing blow. The werewolf struck the floor behind Fymurip, recovered quickly, and came at him once again.

This time, Fymurip was not so clever, not so lucky. A big paw reached out and struck him on the forearm. He shielded himself from the blow with his kilij sword. That softened the strike a little, but even so, Fymurip could feel the trickle of his own blood. The strike stung too, and he wondered if Spanish werewolves were poisonous or infected with rabies. He prayed to Allah that they were not, ducked a second paw swipe, and fell back into a better defensive position.

His plan was to allow the beast to attack, and attack, and attack, until it wore itself out. He'd seen it many times in Starybogow: creatures such as this throwing themselves over and over against a wall, only to find themselves bashed and bloody. Could such a tactic work with this creature? Fymurip hoped so, for he knew that he could not match it move for move. It was too tall, its reach too long, to be able to get in under its natural defenses. In this case, its defense was to attack, to create such a dervish of whirling arms and legs and claws and teeth that its opponent just couldn't cope. And it was doing well.

It was all Fymurip could do to keep from being ripped to shreds. The werewolf attacked, and Fymurip countered, moving slightly left, then right, stabbing where he could, slashing where he might. Death by a thousand cuts, they called it, and precious minutes ticked away as they fought in the tiny, dark space of the corridor, Fymurip moving subtly to put himself on the staircase side of the brawl. But the creature was smart, knew instinctively to keep himself between Fymurip and whatever it was it protected. It went on like that for a long while.

Then Fymurip made a mistake. He dodged left when he should have ducked down. He took a big paw across his shoulder. The blow knocked him back, and his dagger fell from his hand.

He slid across the smooth floor, away from the werewolf. He turned and slid-crawled towards his blade, but the beast kicked it further out of reach. Fymurip flipped over onto his back and lashed out with his sword, catching the werewolf on the snout, peeling back dark skin and drawing blood. The beast howled, shook its face to clear away blood seeping into its eyes. Then it grabbed Fymurip by the shirt and lifted him up, like a doll, and slammed him against the wall.

The strike nearly forced his sword to drop, but Fymurip kept it held, turned it in hand, and slammed its hilt again and again into the beast's throat. The blows were glancing, however, and so the werewolf kept its hold, and kept slamming him into the wall.

Fymurip knew he could not endure much more. The beast was weakening, indeed. Those thousand cuts had done their job, but if it didn't fall soon, they would meet their deaths together.

Then he caught the glint of firelight out of the corner of his eye. A spot on the wall flickered as if it were in flames. Fymurip hammered his sword hilt into the throat of the werewolf and pushed it back enough to shift his body towards the flicker, and he saw that it wasn't the wall itself that was on fire. The light was coming from a perfectly shaped square hole, a chute, that led down somewhere through the wall.

Fymurip pushed his whole weight out against the werewolf, and it fell back a few paces, giving him room to look into the chute. The light was coming from wherever the chute ended, and the smells from the hole were far more inviting than the sweaty, odorous stench emanating from the beast itself.

The werewolf balled up its paw and struck out towards Fymurip's head. He moved just in time to let the beast's knuckles crack against the wall. It howled in pain, and Fymurip pushed it back again, this time gaining real distance between them.

He turned and leapt into the chute, headfirst, not caring about finding his dagger. If the choice was between life and losing a blade, he'd lose the blade. There were other knives to be had in the wide-open world.

But he held his sword tightly and slid down, down, straight through the wall. The light at the bottom grew brighter as he fell. He closed his eyes to it and braced for impact.

His fall did not end in him slamming against another floor, as he expected. The chute ended at floor level, and instead, Fymurip slid across roughly hewn bricks, tearing flesh and clothing as he slid. He gritted his teeth against the pain as he came to a halt. There was silence, and he lay there a moment to soak it in, to catch his breath, to rest. Oh, how wonderful it would be to close his eyes and sleep. And he considered doing just that, his arms and legs exhausted, torn, and aching from the fight. How wonderful sleep would be.

But no rest for the weary, as they say, for as soon as Fymurip caught his breath, he also caught a fresh whiff of the werewolf.

He rolled over and stared through the faint light towards the chute. And there stood the beast, lousy with bleeding cuts, licking its lips, baring its sharp teeth, and moving towards him.

*****

Catherine often wondered if her life would be easier if she just gave in to her father's wishes, married some prince, and had royal children. There would certainly be some kind of stability to that agreement, but what fun would it be? She figured very little and had come to that conclusion many times over in the last three years. But it was moments like this, as she drew her sword and drove it through the breastbone of an unsuspecting guard, that made her question her life choices. Marry and have children, or swordplay? Catherine pulled her sword free and smacked the man down with the broad side of the blade.

Swordplay was so much more fun.

There was a freedom, a sense of purpose, when she fought a foe, something that she could not imagine feeling howling in pain in a birthing chair, while her arrogant husband paced outside the door, if he stood outside it at all, praying that it be a son, and wondering, even before the girl baby gasped her first breath, what foreign prince could take her off his hands when she came of age. Catherine vowed never to allow her children to be used in such a manner, and that's why it made more sense to forgo her betrothal and pick up the sword. The decision had proven successful so far, and as she stepped over the dead guardsman, wiping her bloody blade on the sleeve of his white jerkin, she vowed never to question her decisions again. Until, of course, the next time she questioned her decisions.

She did not consider the guard a foe in the strict sense. If anything, he was a countryman, and a relatively brave one, for he had come out of a corner to block her path, not knowing what fate would bring him in the end. A dedicated servant to the Ezpeletas, for sure, and just another body that she had left behind. How many was that now? Over the past three years, she had lost count. But it was worth it if she could reach the brawl that was happening on the second floor, above her head. She could hear the back and forth, though it was unclear, muffled. She just couldn't get to it. At least not cleanly. Finally, she found a stairway up that was not guarded, and she took it, her soft boots falling quietly on each step. The sounds of the fight had diminished, and for a moment, Catherine's heart ached. Was Fymurip dead? Have mercy, she hoped not. She hoped that her brief pause to kill the guard was not the reason for his fall, for she would never forgive herself if her momentary pause found him dead. But as she reached the top step, she rejoiced. No one was there.

There were certainly signs, however, of a fight, and a right nasty one too. Blood everywhere: the floor, the walls. Tiny pieces of flesh still attached to chunks of fur. Dog fur? Perhaps, but Catherine had seen this kind of fur before, though at the moment, she could not place it. And most of the blood wasn't human, not exactly. She was certain of that. Blood from creatures, especially those of the supernatural variety, smelled differently than human blood. It had a stronger iron smell to it, with a touch of something difficult to describe. Almost cherry in its presentation, like a fermented wine. She suspected that the smell came from the very supernatural elements that formed the creature. She was glad that most of the evidence left behind was not Fymurip's.

Then she saw it. Fymurip's khanjar dagger, beautiful in its repose, its gold inlaid pommel speckled with blood, its curved blade smeared in gore. It just lay there in the corridor as if it were a fruit fallen from a tree. She picked it up, hefted it in her hand. It didn't quite have the right balance for her hand, though she could see why Fymurip liked it. The curved blade could do so much damage twisting and turning through a belly. It was a wonderful weapon, a deadly one. But where was Fymurip?

Further down the corridor she saw a flicker of light flush against a wall. She went to it and found a chute going down. She leaned over into the chute, turning her ear down.

More sounds of struggle, although muted. It must be a long fall, Catherine thought. Fymurip and whatever it was he was fighting must be down there. And if the fight had gone so badly that he had left his dagger behind, it most certainly was not going well wherever he was now. She could hear two separate voices down the chute, and the human one was not very strong. Fymurip was being choked. Had to be.

Catherine backed away from the chute. She looked left, then right, ensuring that no other guards were witness to what she was about to do. Her luck was holding. She straightened her clothing and fixed her belt so that it would not snag going down the chute. Then she leaned forward, Fymurip's dagger pointed out like a needle. She took a deep breath, said a small silent prayer, then leaped into the chute head-first.

VIII

Fymurip held up his legs to shield his body against the raging were-wolf. There was a desperation in its movements, an anger that it had not shown in the corridor above. It was desperate now, and it knew that if it didn't win the fight soon, those thousand cuts would bring it down. It was tiring, Fymurip could see, even though it tried to hide its exhaustion. The beast was overcompensating for the loss of blood, trying to seem more savage and powerful than it really was, and all Fymurip had to do was to bide his time.

But how was that possible without a small blade to parry attacks? Even in its weakened state, the werewolf was formidable, and in a small space like the one they were in, using a sword would be difficult.

They were in a gaol room, and the small corridor that they were in was lined with thick, cold walls on one side, and iron bars on the other. Three, perhaps four, gaols, all dark and brooding. There was light in two sconces on the wall, and Fymurip wished that he could reach out and grab one of their torches. Fire would make a good weapon right now. But the beast was on him, and so he fought for his life.

He kicked the werewolf in the snout, again and again, as he tried fighting off huge paws reaching out for his face in long sweeps. Luckily, the space they were in was narrow, and the beast, in its rage, kept striking the bars as it reached back to take another swipe. It was doing more damage to itself than to Fymurip, but that didn't mean the fight was nearing its end.

The beast weighed a good two hundred fifty pounds, perhaps more, and in the small space, Fymurip found it difficult to fend off every blow. It also snapped at his face with snarled teeth, inches from his eyes. Fymurip could smell the werewolf's breath, feel little droplets of spit on his chin. He gagged and tried pushing the toothy snout away.

The werewolf took advantage of Fymurip's exposed neck, reached down and wrapped both hands around his throat. What powerful hands it had, despite its growing weakness. It squeezed and squeezed, and Fymurip tried prying its fingers free. He could not. He struck at the beast's face, hoping to break a fang or two. He struck hard enough to loosen a few, but the beast kept squeezing.

Fymurip gasped for air. He could feel his life slipping away, and he began to panic. He did not want to die in a cold, dark gaol room in Spain; that was not how it was supposed to go with him. He was supposed to die on the field of battle, rushing a line of Christian knights or standing firm against a charging horde of barbarians. All in the service of a sultan, for the honor of Allah. He kept trying to break free from the werewolf's grip, but it was no use. He could not breathe any longer. He couldn't remember the last time he had taken a breath.

He closed his eyes and waited for the end.

A rush of air swept over him, and something crashed into the back of the werewolf, knocking it forward, and dislodging its fingers from his neck. Fymurip gasped for air and rolled to the right.

He rubbed his aching throat. He blinked blurry eyes and tried to make out the shape that was on top of the beast, driving a blade deep into its spine.

"Catherine?"

She looked at him as she turned the blade one final time. Fymurip heard a snap, and the beast stopped thrashing.

He pulled himself up into a sitting position and leaned against the wall. He coughed several times, took deep breaths. He was sore from head to toe. "What are you doing here?"

Catherine pulled his khanjar dagger from the beast's back, walked over to him, and dropped it in his lap. "Saving your skin," she said, "as I always do."

*****

"I had it right where I wanted it," Fymurip said, slowly rising while rubbing his neck. He gripped the dagger and checked the blade. Bloody, but sharp. "I was playing with it."

"Indeed, you were." Catherine looked around the room. "Where are we?"

Fymurip shook his head. "I do not know. A gaol room, perhaps the dungeon." He walked over to her; his expression confused. "What are you doing here? We agreed that you'd stay out of the castle."

Catherine fixed her belt and rubbed her face. "Lucky for you I didn't."

"How did you get in?"

Catherine shrugged. "Through the front gate."

He blanched. "The front—the—"

"I hid under a wagon," she said, putting her hand gently on his chest. "Calm yourself. It wasn't difficult."

Fymurip shook his head. "You were spotted. I know you were."

"Not that I could tell, though it's best that we find our way out of here and continue with our mission. I can't imagine that the castle will continue to stay ignorant of our presence."

"Our mission? Our mission was for you to not be involved, Catherine. You're here. You are now involved."

Fymurip could see her expression change. To guilt, perhaps? Anger? The girl could easily hide her true feelings. "I'm involved. I've been involved since we arrived in Spain. No denying that. What will happen... will. Now let's get out of here and continue."

"Yes," said a voice from down the row of gaol cells. "Please do, so that I can sleep."

Fymurip turned, held his dagger forward. Catherine drew her sword. They stepped out of the shadows together and moved towards the voice. "Who are you?" Fymurip asked. "Speak up!"

"I was trying to sleep, and when Miguel left, I hoped that I could. But your incessant blathering is keeping me from my dreams."

"Who is Miguel?" Catherine asked.

From the darkness of the last gaol cell, a small green face emerged. It was like a child's face, but wider, and its wrinkles clearly indicated old age. The person, or whatever it was, smiled, revealing straight, but broken teeth. It wrapped two small hands around the bars of its cell and pressed itself against those bars. It wore a simple shiff of grey torn in a few places, and it looked as if someone had tried to stitch up the tears to minimal effect. The creature was thin, but not weak, or at least it didn't appear to be. Fymurip could see the outline of some muscle on the creature's arms.

"Miguel was the Lobisome that you just killed," it said. "He was guarding me, though I do not know why. How something as small as me requires a guard like that, I cannot say. But I'm glad that you—"

"I know what you are," Catherine said, and Fymurip could hear the hostility in her voice. "You are a Trasgo. An Asturian goblin. A deceitful little wretch that requires two Lobisome to guard him. I now regret having killed it."

The Trasgo seemed insulted by Catherine's accusations. It backed off an inch, its tiny mouth shaped in a perfect O. "Madam, you insult me. I assure you, I'm nothing more than a simple thief, like yourself I would imagine."

"Why are you here?"

"Thieving," it said, putting up its hands as if the question was obvious. "I was caught, but not until I had a sack of goods. Oh, this castle is ripe with treasure, if you know where to find it. I was almost out the gate when they grabbed me." Its shoulders dropped. It looked so dejected. "I'm such a failure. I should be beaten, flogged, pulled on the rack."

Catherine swiped her sword across the bars. Sparks flew. "Shut up! We don't have time to banter with you." She turned to Fymurip. "Let us go. The castle will not stay silent for long. We have to find Tizona now, and—"

"Tizona? You seek that sword?"

"What do you know of it?" Fymurip asked.

"I told you: I'm a thief. Oh, I would never presume to think I am worthy to steal such an exalted treasure as Tizona." It moved back up to the bars. It smiled. "But I know where it is."

Catherine shrugged. "So, do we. In the throne room."

"Oh, no, young lady. That is too dangerous a place for a trinket like Tizona to reside. Too many ways to get there. It is in Ezpeleta's personal quarters. And I know how to get there without guards seeing me."

They paused, and even Catherine seemed to be considering the creature's offer. For surely he was making one.

"You want us to free you," Fymurip said, "so that you may help us find Tizona? Scheme carefully, whomever you are. We just killed a Lobisome. A small goblin like yourself would be no work at all."

The Trasgo nodded. "Indeed, and I understand that. Free me, and I will take you to Tizona. I will be your slave if you wish it."

Catherine swiped the bars again with her sword. The goblin shrieked and fell into the far corner of its cell. "I said shut up. We will not free you, beast. There is nothing you can say that we can trust."

"Catherine," Fymurip said, touching her lightly on her sword arm. "Let's think of it for a moment. If this creature is telling the truth and Tizona is not in the throne room, then we are going to have to stay longer in the castle than we wish, seeking out Ezpeleta's personal quarters. I think I know where they are from the map, but I cannot be sure. It could take twice as long, and most certainly, his personal quarters will be guarded far better than anything we have encountered so far." He leaned in and whispered. "What risk do we have of freeing a little goblin?"

"A great risk," Catherine said. "You are not from Spain, my friend. You do not know this creature like I do. Trasgos are deceitful. It might lead us into a trap."

Fymurip nodded. "Yes, but I have been led into many, and I have always gotten free. I don't see what other choice can be made. But you are right. I am not from Spain. This is your country. It is your decision."

Catherine sighed and looked back and forth between Fymurip and the Trasgo. Finally, she shook her head, and said, "Very well. But the minute it deceives, I'll gut it."

Fymurip nodded. "And I'll assist." He moved to the cell, placed his dagger behind the lock on the bars, and snapped it open. The goblin was leery at first to step out. Slowly, it did.

When the Trasgo stood straight, the top of its head reached Fymurip's belt. Now he could see that the creature had a small tuft of black hair on the back of its head, tied tightly with a piece of old cord. Its eyes were darker than they had first appeared. He had no white in his eyes, and he gave off a smell that was, this close, unsavory. Not as foul as some creatures Fymurip had encountered in his days, but bad enough.

Fymurip stepped back, held his dagger forward. "Now, move slowly, and take us to Tizona."

The goblin bowed humbly. "This way."

It led them up the chute. It was difficult for both Fymurip and Catherine to find sufficient purchase to make the climb, but the goblin was patient. It kept stopping and offering a hand to aid Catherine as they ascended. Catherine refused to take it.

Finally, they reached the hall in which Fymurip had battled the Lobisome. "This way," the goblin said.

As they followed, Fymurip asked, "What is your name?"

The creature looked at him with its coal-black eyes and smiled. "I am Alfredo."

IX

IX

Alfredo took them on a long route around the castle and down to the first floor. Alfredo was small, so he was more easily cloaked in the shadows they used to avoid detection. Catherine and Fymurip were not, so they had to pause more often than practical, wait for calm, and then continue on. Catherine kept a wary eye on the little cretin, knowing that, at any moment, it could run off or sound an alarm. She didn't think that they had much time anyway. No proof in the air. Just a feeling.

"Stay close," she warned Alfredo more than once. "I'm watching you."

By Catherine's account, they had moved to the opposite side of the castle. Alfredo had done as promised. But that wasn't unusual for a Trasgo. A Trasgo believed that it could do anything, and when given a task, it would always try hard to move heaven and earth to fulfill that task, or so the legend told. The problem wasn't their service, but afterwards, when you just wanted the thing to go away. It always found some excuse to stay in your employment. Catherine sighed and made a mental note to consider ordering it to drown itself at some point. Would it harm itself on order? She did not know, but it was worthy of thought.

They ducked through an archway that led into what looked like an old kitchen, with dust-covered wooden chairs and a half-broken table. Old meal sacks and discarded broom handles and chopping blocks. Rusty hooks for meat. Cobwebs and rats. A lot of barrels and crates were stacked against the wall, and they looked new, fresh. Clearly, this tiny room served as storage now, and it made sense that Alfredo would know of such a place. It could serve a little goblin like himself for quite a while. The rats alone would make good meals on cold nights.

"Why are we here?" Catherine asked as they entered the room.

"Shh!" Alfredo said, putting a knobby finger against his green puckered lips. "Look up."

They did, and amidst a tangle of cobwebs and spiders, lay a trap door. Catherine almost missed it, the only light in the room coming from the door sitting ajar to the hallway. The trap door lay flush against the wooden slats and joints of the ceiling. Catherine squinted. It looked like the only thing keeping it shut was a small bolt latch, and it was rusty.

"It doesn't look like it's been used in a while," Fymurip said.

Alfredo nodded. "I have never seen Ezpeleta take kitchen help into his bed chamber, but someone used to, his father or grandfather perhaps, and that door was used for such clandestine meetings. Over the years, it has been forgotten, covered on the other side as it is with a thick carpet. I don't believe anyone alive knows it exists, including Ezpeleta, or they would have sealed it shut by now. But if we go through there… we find your sword."

Catherine was reluctant to trust the table underneath as the way up. It could support Alfredo's weight, but not hers, and certainly not Fymurip's.

They pushed it out of the way and stacked three crates high, supported by heavy barrels. When they were finished, Catherine turned to Alfredo and grabbed him by the neck. "You will go up first, and you will then open the door in full. Do you understand?" Alfredo, his eyes watering, his mouth aquiver, nodded. "I promise. I am yours to serve."

She let him go, and he moved, hand over hand, up the pile, ripping the cobwebs away as he ascended. The rust on the bolt latch made it difficult to open, but he fiddled with the mechanism until it gave.

At first, Alfredo just crouched there, his head against the door, listening. Made sense, Catherine supposed, though every move the Trasgo made must be questioned. Then it pushed up against the door with its shoulder, letting its creak sound, then settle, sound and settle. The carpet above it shielded any light in the room, though Catherine could see a faint sliver of it. The room was lit, there was no doubt. Was there an occupant?

Alfredo opened the door just enough to crawl through. He slipped up and through the gap like a snake crawling through a crack in a stone wall. There was silence, and more silence, and more, until Catherine began to worry.

"He's betrayed us!" She hissed. "Let's leave him."

Fymurip put up his hand. "Patience. One more moment."

But Catherine could see that Fymurip, despite his willingness to wait, held his dagger firm, ready for anything.

They waited a minute more. Then the carpet was pulled away from the hole, and lamplight spread across their faces. Alfredo's green, misshapen head appeared. He motioned with an anxious grey-green hand. "Come, come," he whispered. "There is no one here."

"You first?" Fymurip asked.

Catherine nodded. If this was a trap, she was willing to take the brunt of it. This was her mission, her country.

She moved up slowly, making sure her feet were secure for the next step. Fymurip placed his hands on her thighs for support. She liked his hands there. They were strong, steady. "Thank you," she said, and tried to keep her mind on the task at hand.

She put her head through the hole. She looked around. It was a small room, smaller than she would have imagined Ezpeleta having as his personal quarters. But it was empty, save for Alfredo who stood near a fireplace.

"Come," he said, still whispering, as if there was someone in the room.

Catherine double-checked. No one. Faint light, a musty smell of dust and age, but no one. So she pulled herself up, scooted away from the hole, then motioned for Fymurip to follow.

When he was securely in the room, they joined Alfredo at the mantel.

The Trasgo raised a lit candle, and Catherine's eyes followed the flame up until they rested on a long, broad blade fixed to a lacquered plaque.

"Tizona!"

*****

It was beautiful, if a little simple. A long steel blade, three feet at least, its fuller about half that length, its central ridge running the rest. Its point was fine. Its pommel was shaped almost like a family crest. Its grip was black worn leather. Its steel cross-guard curved like wilting leaves. It rested on two modest hooks that had been drilled into the castle rock. Its scabbard lay on the mantel. Both were covered with dust, though not much. It was clear to Fymurip that housekeepers kept the blade relatively clean.

He wanted it immediately, though it was a little larger than the swords he fought with. Tizona was more like a Gunwald Sword, like Lux's sword, and if the knight were here, there'd be no doubt as to who would take it. Fymurip was tall enough to reach up and seize it; the other two were not.

"What are you waiting for?" Catherine asked. "Take it."

"Of course."

Fymurip reached up on tiptoes, grabbed the scabbard first. And then he strained to grip the handle. He held it tight and removed it from its hooks carefully.

In his mind, he heard the word "Colada," and a savage nausea gripped his body.

He almost fell. Catherine and Alfredo grabbed him. He dropped Tizona, and its strike against the floor echoed across the room.

"Are you ill?" Catherine asked.

It took him a moment to respond, but slowly, slowly, the room stopped spinning, his stomach stopped churning. The desire to vomit subsided, and he said, "Yes, I am okay. Did you hear that?"

"Hear what?"

"That name. When I gripped the sword, I heard a name."

"What name?" Catherine asked.

"Colada."

He could not hear it now, and obviously neither Catherine nor Alfredo could either. So strange, and he wondered if he were imagining things.

He pulled away from them and gained his feet. He breathed deeply, gathered himself, reached down and picked up the sword again.

Nausea struck him, but this time, he did not let go, though the room spun. And all he could hear in his mind was "Colada, Colada, Colada," over and over again.

"Colada," Fymurip said. "Can you hear it?"

"No," Catherine barked. "Drop the sword!"

He dropped it. Like before, the room stopped spinning, and he returned to normal. Fymurip looked at Catherine's expression. She looked worse than he felt.

"What is that name I keep hearing?" he asked. "Tell me what 'Colada' means."

"Colada is El Cid's other sword," Alfredo said in a yipping tone. "It is El Cid's other sword."

Fymurip looked sternly at Catherine. "You did not tell me the man had two swords."

Catherine shook her head, concern spread across her lips. "I did not think it was an issue. We were ordered to find Tizona. Why would Colada come into it? I don't know much about Colada."

"Well," Fymurip said, pointing at Tizona lying almost peaceful on the cold floor, "that thing is cursed, and it keeps repeating Colada over and over. You take it and see if it does the same."

Catherine hesitated. "Very well," she said, then reached down and grabbed the hilt.

The sword was heavy for her, but she gripped the handle and tried to straighten. Her eyes rolled into the back of her head. She dropped the sword. Fymurip and Alfredo caught and lowered her to the floor.

"Do you see?"

Catherine nodded. "Yes. I can hear the name. But I can't hold that sword. Neither can you. How are we going to take it out of the castle?"

Fymurip grabbed the scabbard. "Let's try to put it in the scabbard and see if that helps."

Gritting his teeth, he quickly grabbed the sword and pushed it into the scabbard with Alfredo's help. He let go of the handle, took a breath, then grabbed the scabbard. The extra layer helped. The nausea was lessened, but still there, and in quantities that he had no desire to have with him on the long journey back to Germany. He could still hear 'Colada' strong and clear in his mind. If anything, the call had grown stronger.

"I can't abide by its incessant babble of that name," Fymurip said. "Why on earth is it screaming for Colada?"
Catherine shook her head, stood. "I don't know. What do you know of it, Trasgo?"

Alfredo had been picking things off the carpet as they had struggled with the sword. He looked up, surprised. "I know nothing of Colada beyond who owned it. El Cid, yes, he is the one whom it belonged to. But I know nothing else. Perhaps Tizona is lonely and longs for its partner."

"Did El Cid fight with both swords at the same time?" Fymurip asked. He was beginning to like this fabled Spanish warrior.

"I don't know," Catherine replied. "Perhaps not hand in hand like you do your dagger and sword, but in some capacity together."

"What do you know of its history?"

Catherine considered. She took longer than he wanted. It was not wise to linger here in Ezpeleta's quarters, but what else could he do? He had to know as much as possible before they moved any further. "If I remember my stories as a child, El Cid gave Colada to one of his knights. I do not know which one."

"Do you know where it is?" Fymurip asked.

"No."

"I do," Alfredo said, grinning ear to ear. "It is in your father's Royal Alcazar in Madrid."

"Wait a moment," Fymurip said, taking a step towards the little goblin. "I thought you said you knew nothing of the sword."

"I don't," Alfredo said, backing away. "I know nothing about the sword. But I know where it is. There is a difference, brave sir, in knowing about something and knowing where it resides. It is in the Royal Alcazar."

"What are we going to do?" Catherine asked.

Fymurip considered. Neither he nor Catherine could hold it, much less carry it. Perhaps the effects would be lessened even more if it simply hung on their backs, or at their belts. But Catherine was too short to have a three-foot sword dangling at her side. And Fymurip was not about to put it on his belt. Then he had a thought.

"You grip it," he said to Alfredo.

"Me, sir?"

"Yes, you. Put the grip in your hand. Now."

Alfredo nodded obediently, cautiously slipped past Fymurip, and did as he was told. He lay down on the floor and carefully wrapped his hands around the handle.

Nothing, at least nothing that Fymurip could see. The creature looked well. He did not breathe poorly; his color remained the same. Alfredo opened his eyes and turned his head. "Is this okay, sir?"

Fymurip nodded. "Yes, that is fine. So, you will carry the sword for us. Apparently, it does not affect you like it—"

"He cannot carry the sword," Catherine said, jumping into view. "That is madness. We cannot let that cretin hold the sword. He'll steal it the minute we leave the castle. He'll—"

But her argument was cut short by a sharp bleat of a horn. The alarm had been sounded.

X

"**W**e must go now," Fymurip said, grabbing the sword by its scabbard, braving the nausea, and bow-slinging it onto Alfredo's back.

"How can he carry it?" Catherine said. "Look at him: he's doubled over like a bovine."

And so he was. The weight of Tizona on the goblin's back looked almost comical. He was a beast of burden, for sure, with that blade on his back. He tried but could not stand upright. Tizona was too long. He'd have to port it like a mule.

"It is fine," Alfredo said, falling onto all fours. "I prefer to travel with hands and feet both."

"I said let's go!"

Catherine went down the trap door first, followed by Alfredo, who was handed down by Fymurip. No nausea came to him holding the creature's arms, praise Allah. That, at least, was hopeful. In a desperate situation - like they were in now - it was nice to know that they could scoop Alfredo up and move quickly if necessary and have no worries about health. Fymurip handed him down, and Catherine took him.

Fymurip followed, swinging himself out and away from the crates that they had piled up. "Follow me," he said, ignoring Alfredo's motion to take a left out of the storeroom. "You follow me, or I'll carry you."

Alfredo followed, and Catherine took the rear.

They crossed the courtyard, keeping to the shadows as best as possible. "Where are we going?" Catherine asked.

"To get my grapple," Fymurip said.

He had tucked it away under bushes, and he hoped that it was still there. The alarm had been sounded either by finding his gear or the dead body of the werewolf and their goblin prisoner missing. The latter was the most likely reason.

He reached his hiding place, and there it lay coiled, like he had left it. He scooped it up, turned, and headed towards the stone stairway off the courtyard that he had seen when he had dropped over the ramparts on entry. It had been guarded by two men, but hopefully the alarm had moved them away. As he led them, he could hear men shouting orders, in Spanish. He looked back at Catherine for translation, but she shook her head, obviously incapable of understanding their muffled voices.

Fymurip turned a corner and headed towards the stone stairway. And two men, in chainmail hauberks, carrying short swords and shields, rounded the next corner. Fymurip pulled his blades and laid into them.

They were swift with their shields, holding them up quickly to deflect his initial strike. But the dagger found a seam through their chainmail defense and gutted the closest man. He lurched forward and dropped his shield. He clutched his bloody wound and fell down.

Alfredo jumped on the legs of the other guard like a cat and bit down hard on his thigh. The man screamed and shook his leg, trying to free it from the goblin. He tried holding his shield up as well, to deflect Fymurip's attack. He tried stabbing out at Fymurip, but he lost his balance and fell back against the stone stairway. Fymurip let him fall, then stepped up, waited a moment, then drew his sword swiftly across the man's throat.

"Let him go," he said to Alfredo. "He's dead."

"There are more coming," Catherine said, pointing behind them at a line of other guards that were entering the courtyard.

An arrow struck the stone stairway and shattered. Fymurip grabbed the scruff of Alfredo's shiff and pulled him up the stairway.

More arrows hit the stones as they ascended, but none found skin.

Two flights later and they were on the second floor and heading towards the rampart where Fymurip had entered. As they ran, arrows struck the bricks around them, and men began climbing the stairs. Guards, too, were on the other side of the castle, on the second floor.

"We're being surrounded," Catherine said. "We have to go over now!"

She was right, but Fymurip didn't like it. He wanted to reach his entry point. He knew it, and it was always best to retreat through familiar passages. But there was no time. They had to leave the castle now.

He stopped and unraveled his rope and grapple. He took the hook and stabbed it into the rampart, in the space between bricks where the mortar was softest. It took three strikes, but the point of the hook found purchase, Fymurip threw the rope over the side.

An arrow struck the wall nearest, ricocheted, and clipped Alfredo's face. The little beast yelped. Fymurip placed his hand on the goblin's head, said, "Be still. It's only a scratch." Then he turned to Catherine. "You go first."

She nodded and sheathed her sword, and Fymurip helped her take the rope. He watched her repel down the wall until she was halfway down, then he turned to Alfredo. "You next."

The goblin did not argue, He nodded profusely and held up his arms as if he were a little baby. Fymurip scooped him up and placed him over the side, secured his tiny hands on the rope, and let him go. "Hold tight, or you won't survive the fall."

Alfredo scuttled down the rope, hand under hand, as if he had done it many times, and he found the ground almost immediately after Catherine landed.

Fymurip turned and deflected the sword strike of a guard who had caught up. The man was surprised at how quickly his target recovered and defended. He screamed at Fymurip in Spanish, a curse probably. Fymurip could not understand most of it, but the word "Tizona" came through loud and clear. And not from the sword. This man knew what had been taken from the castle. They all did, most likely.

Fymurip leaned back to dodge a club strike, gripped the handle of his sword tightly, and punched the guard across the face. Blood and a chipped tooth flew out of the man's mouth, and Fymurip followed with his dagger across the man's face, drawing blood from his eyes. Fymurip drove his boot into the man's chest and pushed him back.

He sheathed his sword, grabbed the rope, and flung himself over the battlement.

*****

Catherine and Alfredo had moved away from the castle and towards the lip of the front gate bridge. There, they would find some protection behind the stone railing, but neither had a bow with which to provide counter-fire against the arrows shot towards Fymurip as he repelled down the wall. Catherine worried that he was dropping too fast, that he would hit the ground and damage his legs, twist his knees. But the Tatar moved expertly, using the darkness to cover his descent. One of the guards on the rampart reached over to cut the rope from the grapple. He was successful.

Fymurip had anticipated such a move and braced himself for the fall. He bent his knees at the right moment to cushion the blow, then rolled. A swarm of arrows struck the ground where he had struck.

"Over here!" Catherine shouted.

Fymurip made little hops like a baby goat to avoid missile fire. He also bounced left and right, not giving the guard archers an easy target. Catherine was impressed. She smiled.

Fymurip hit the ground and slid until he was next to Catherine. "What now?" he asked.

Catherine looked for an escape. "Through the town."

She could see that Fymurip wanted to argue the point, but he kept his mouth shut and nodded. "You lead the way."

Now she was in the lead, and she had no idea where to go. She knew where they had placed their horses, and eventually—assuming that they were not caught in flight—they'd work their way back to them. But right now, they needed to just go, to flee, to move, to get as far away from the castle as possible. The only way that she could see was straight through the town.

So, they ran, up the ditch bank, using the bridge to cover their movement. When they reached the top, Catherine ran straight down the street which led into Marcilla.

Behind them, she could hear the castle gate open. And she knew what that meant. More guards, perhaps even ones on horses, would be in pursuit. She was not concerned with her and Fymurip's ability to handle any threat. But with the Trasgo in tow, the situation was less than perfect, though the little cretin didn't seem to be losing any energy. He trundled along behind her at pace, keeping one hand on Tizona to ensure its safety.

Her biggest concern were the townsfolk. Marcilla was coming alive with candle and lamplight flickering in windows. The commotion at the castle was beginning to rouse people from their sleep. Would they help or hinder their escape? It was unlikely that they would aid, so the best thing to do was to run as fast as possible, and then find a place to hide, for days if necessary.

The town was not very large, and so they reached the end of it quickly. Catherine could hear the castle guards behind her, making far more noise than they should, but coming on strong.

"We have to get our horses," Fymurip said. "It's the only way."

Catherine nodded. She turned right and headed down the road on the outskirts of the town, more of a small rutted dirt path that led behind several mercantile establishments. "I know," Catherine replied. "Which way do we turn to get there?"

"You don't know?"

She could hear shock and frustration in Fymurip's voice. "I'm busy at the moment. I've turned too many corners. I'm not sure now."

"Let me help," Alfredo said. He stopped and pointed towards the back door of one of the shops they were passing.

Catherine halted, nodded towards the door. "What's in there?"

"Nothing," Alfredo said, "but our safety. Come."

Catherine gave Fymurip a long stare. The Tatar shrugged. "Up to you."

She nodded reluctantly. Alfredo smiled and took the lead.

The door was locked. Fymurip popped it open with his dagger, and they went in.

It was dark. The air was lousy with the scent of oil and candlewax. There did not appear to be an occupant. Perhaps it was a shop for a candlestick maker, a lamplighter. Perhaps both. When they were in, Alfredo took them by their hands and led them to a place behind a large iron vat, still warm from the day's melting. He pressed his bony finger against his lips. "Shhh! Make no sound, and I will make them go away."

The goblin went back to the door. He closed it till there was only a small crack. He peered through that crack and waited.

Soon, the guards in pursuit were outside the door. Catherine put her hand on her sword. Fymurip did the same, though he had never sheathed his dagger. It lay waiting in his hand to strike if necessary. She hoped that he didn't need to use it on the Trasgo, but it was looking more and more necessary as the minutes ticked past. *The little cretin has led us to our deaths,* she thought. *There is no way out of this place.*

She could hear the guards outside the door.

"Where did they go?" one asked.

"I know not," another answered. "They could not have left Marcilla; we would have seen. They are in one of these buildings, I'm sure. Let's check them."

With that, Alfredo waved his hand across the crack and smooth red smoke trickled from his fingers. It coiled itself around the door, and like a hand, closed it shut.

The guard outside stopped in front of the closed door and pressed his face against the window. It was too dark for him to see in very far, though a sliver of moonlight cast a narrow beam across the dusty wooden floor. Alfredo was as still as stone beside the door. Catherine and Fymurip did the same.

The guard lingered for a few minutes more, seemingly mesmerized, near catatonic. It was hard to see details on his face, but Catherine was sure that he was grinning, as if he were watching a funny puppet show through the stained glass of the door. Then he turned and walked away.

When the guards' voices fell into the distance, Catherine emerged from behind the vat. She grabbed Alfredo's scruff, said, "What did you do?"

Alfredo shook his head. "Nothing sinister, I assure you. A simple lock spell, which makes the person or persons wanting to enter turn away and forget everything. We are safe now. They will not try to search this shop again. We stay here till morning, and then we can slip away, quietly, and no one will know."

"And you never bothered to use this spell when you were in the castle's gaol?" Fymurip asked.

"It only works on inanimate objects, like locks, doors, and the like. And it only affects people, not creatures like me or Miguel. So, you see, they were very clever in using a werewolf as my guard. And it would have been silly to use a locking spell on my own cell."

"Quiet!" Catherine said, letting him go and stepping back a few paces. She put her hands on her hips, breathed deeply, and said, "I have to think. I need time to think."

"About what?" Fymurip asked.

"About everything," she said.

"Are we going after Colada?"

Fymurip's question startled her. She hadn't really considered that as an option. "Why would we do that?"

Fymurip sheathed his dagger and pointed to Tizona still resting in its scabbard on Alfredo's back. "That sword keeps calling its name. Clearly, they are connected in some way."

Catherine shook her head. "We were charged with finding Tizona and returning it to Germany. That is all I am prepared to do."

"Yes, you are correct. Our mission was to find Tizona, and we have done that. But if the League is unaware of Colada, then just acquiring Tizona may not be enough. We may go through all this trouble and, whatever it is that the League is trying to prevent by securing Tizona, may still happen if Colada is allowed to remain in Spain. I was not in support of this mission from the beginning, you know that. I'm still not. But I don't want us to risk blood and treasure only to come up short. You've seen how powerful the Eldar Gods are, Catherine. We may have no choice.

"A young lady once told me that 'we who serve a greater good give our masters what they need, not what they want'. Georg wants Tizona; he may need Colada as well."

Catherine blanched. Throwing my words back at me! She'd known that one day, if she persisted in waxing philosophical, her words would come back to haunt her. She had not imagined that Fymurip would be the one slinging them back. But he was right. There was a connection between the swords. She did not know exactly what that connection was, but clearly Georg did, for the message that he had written her personally was still tucked in her boot. She shook her head. "No. We have done our duty, and I will not risk the mission by going after Colada. Besides, I want to be free of this Trasgo as soon as possible. He'll have to accompany us back to Germany, and then I want to see the back of him. We return to Lübeck at once. We will tell Georg of Colada when we arrive, and we'll let him make the decision to go after it or not."

She could see that Fymurip wanted to argue, but he closed him mouth, nodded patiently, and found a place on the floor to rest. Catherine did the same, keeping a wary eye on Alfredo as he tucked himself into a corner, hugging Tizona as if it were a child. He had done them a good service with the locking spell; he'd saved their lives most likely. But she did not trust him. One, perhaps two, good deeds, could not erase a creature's nature. Alfredo was a Trasgo, a goblin, and he could be nothing else.

As she dozed, Catherine thought of Georg's message. It rang loud and clear in her mind, and she knew exactly what it meant.

Should she tell Fymurip? And why hadn't she already? If she shared the message with him, then he'd understand why it was necessary to return to Lübeck immediately with Tizona. Why keep the truth from him? But Georg had given her the message in confidence. Georg did not want Fymurip to know. Because he was a Tatar, a Muslim? Perhaps. There was no reason why Catherine should keep the message from Fymurip. So, why was she reluctant? If I do, I betray Georg's trust, she thought as she dozed. And I am not prepared to do that, for he's been more of a father to me than my king of a father has ever been. So, she would wait for now and keep the truth of El Cid's swords from her friend and companion, Fymurip Azat. For now, at least.

As she fell asleep, Georg's message played over and over in her mind... *El dragon no puede levantarse...*

The dragon must not rise.

Part Two

The Girls from Zaragoza

I

Catherine slept restless beneath a full moon. She dreamed of storm clouds, multiplying and growing black with rain. She ran through a field - no, down a wide road - away from something. A large shape, dark itself though outlined with filtered light. It was a silhouette, dark as an opal and coming for her. She ran. The road was muddy. She tried seeing where she was going, but the light that illuminated the shape of the creature in pursuit failed to show her path. She was in darkness, feeling the creature following her getting closer, closer, until she could feel heat emanating from its body. And its breath as well, now on her neck, coarse and incessant as if it were made of sand.

Then she was in sand, racing up a hot dune, the sun inescapable like the storm clouds previously. There was too much light now. Her eyes were blinded by the painful white shine of the sun. And she ran. She did not know where, but she knew that the creature was still after her. She turned her head to see the beast, but the light was too great. Just a blurred shape, nothing sharp, refined. A white-hot fog moving towards her, now faster and faster. And she pumped her legs as hard as she could, but the sand was deep, the dune high.

Now she was waist-deep in it, as if she were swimming in an ocean. She slowed, though she tried keeping ahead of the creature. But it grew closer, closer, until again, she could feel its breath on her nape.

There was no escaping it now. She could go no further. So, she turned, drew her sword, and waited.

Lines of sharp teeth flared. A roar. Fire. Then she saw it, as plain as her own face in a mirror. It bared its teeth, reached out for her, and snapped her face away.

She awoke and jumped upright. Her skin was wet, her heart pounded.

Across the dying embers of their small campfire, Fymurip stared at her.

"Are you all right?" he asked.

Catherine breathed deeply, took a moment, and realized it was just a dream. "I'm - fine. Just a dream."

"Must have been a bad one. You were mumbling, and your legs were moving."

"Did I say anything useful?" she asked trying to lighten the mood.

Fymurip shook his head. "Something *levan - levantarse*? I couldn't quite understand it -."

"It's nothing, I'm sure. Just a dream." She looked around the camp.

They were in a small clearing, just south of the French border, heading back to Avignon. They had stopped for the night. But there had been three of them. "Where's that little wretch?"

"Alfredo? He said he was going hunting."

She panicked, raised up on her knees... then saw the sword lying beside the fire, wrapped in a blanket. She sighed, settled, suddenly hearing the word Colada Colada Colada over and over, faint indeed, but there, as it had been the entire trip from Navarre. When it was on Alfredo's back, it calmed. Lying beside the fire, it was again active and audible, and Catherine wondered just how loud it would become if it were shed of its blanket.

"Tizona is safe, Catherine," Fymurip said, poking the fire with a long stick to quicken the embers. "You have nothing to fear."

"I fear nothing," she lied, "but I don't trust that little beast."

"As you have stated time and again," Fymurip said, "and I'm sure will state it some more in the coming weeks. But you better find some peace with him, for he's going to be with us a long time. He's the only one who can carry the sword to Lübeck, and I'm not inclined to play mediator between you two the entire way."

Catherine huffed. "You don't have to do anything, Fymurip. I can take care of myself."

"Of that, I've no doubt. But I don't want to wake up one morning and find our little friend's throat cut ear to ear."

Catherine stood and moved closer to the fire. She picked the last morsels of meat off the charred bones of a rabbit. She chewed them slowly and tossed the carcass into the fire. "Don't worry, my friend. I've never killed anyone I've travelled with."

Fymurip chuckled. "That's good to know." He paused and scooted closer to the fire himself. Catherine watched him. His face seemed to search the flames for something he could not see. "So, are you going to tell me what's bothering you?"

"What do you mean?"

"You are usually very calm, reserved, and steady under pressure. You usually sleep very well. But since Navarre, you've barely slept, and when you do, you dream fitfully, just like now. What is on your mind?"

Everything. "We're on a dangerous mission, Fymurip. Don't you think it's wise to worry?"

He nodded. "I do, and if you were anyone else, I wouldn't give it thought. But you're not any person, Catherine, and you are very close to home. Are you concerned about your father?"

"We aren't that close to Aragon." In truth, they weren't that far either, but she wasn't about to admit it. It wasn't her father that troubled her dreams.

"We're only a few hours ride to France," Fymurip said, "and once we cross the border, your father will not have any way to—"

"It's not my father!" Catherine jumped to her feet, put her hands on her hips, and walked into the darkness away from the fire. "It's that infernal sword," she said, admitting a partial truth this time. "It screams 'Colada Colada Colada' all the time. It won't shut up!"

"Yes, it is a noisy thing. All the more reason to make sure Alfredo stays alive and healthy. He seems to be the only one it calms around."

Catherine shook her head, sighed. "I don't think I can endure it all the way to Germany."

Fymurip paused, then said, "There is another path we can take, Catherine. We can turn around and go after Colada."

She turned and walked back into the firelight. "Oh, yes, of course. Let's go and steal another sword from my father. And this time, let's break into the Royal Alcazar to do it."

"Now you're just being difficult." Fymurip stood and walked around the fire to face her. "If the only way to keep Tizona from driving you mad is to go after its partner, I think it's worth it."

Catherine was about to say something snide again. She paused. She could see in Fymurip's eyes that he was sincere, that he truly had concern about her welfare. That was sweet, and she made a note to thank him for it later. But not now.

"Colada is the last thing we need to go after," she said.

Fymurip leaned in. "Why? What aren't you telling me?"

"Nothing... I..."

"What?"

"Be quiet!" A high-pitched, raspy voice rang out of the darkness. Then a little goblin scampered into the firelight with a squirrel in its left hand. "I could hear you arguing a mile away."

Alfredo dropped his kill near the fire. Catherine took this moment to change the subject. "That's all you could find?"

The Trasgo seemed insulted. His eyes lit up; his jaw dropped open. "It is a plump one. But if you are concerned, my lady, I will not eat. I will just tuck myself away beneath a tree somewhere and live on the sweet smells of squirrel meat roasting—"

Basta! Catherine said, growing annoyed again. "Enough. Stop talking. I cannot endure your voice and Tizona's at the same time."

She could feel Fymurip's eyes on her, but she ignored them, turned away from him, and took a seat beside the fire. She rubbed her arms, not because she was cold, but because it made her feel better. It calmed her from the images of the dream still flashing through her mind.

A bolt struck a burning log next to her.

Fire and sparkling ash flew into the sky from the impact. Catherine rolled left and drew her sword.

She counted twenty men emerging from the woods, wearing hard leather cuirasses over yellow-and-red shirts. Some carried swords, shields. Others had crossbows. They wore a mixture of different helmets, from cabassets, to morions, to thin leather caps. Judging strictly from their makeshift clothing, they were bandits, but Catherine knew better.

"Bandits?" Fymurip asked. He had already drawn his swords and now stood beside her.

"No," she said, as a squadron of five horsemen trotted out of the dark and up to their campsite. "They are my father's men."

*****

"How can you tell?" Fymurip asked.

Catherine pointed to one of the shields the man closest to them was holding. "Four red vertical pallets on a golden field. That's our heraldry."

In all the time he had known her, she had never worn anything symbolizing her house's coat of arms. Made sense, in her line of work. And from her expression now, he could tell that she was not happy seeing the symbol again.

"Do we fight?"

Catherine nodded and stepped to the right. "When I give the signal."

The lead man brought his horse to a halt, paused, then dismounted. Fymurip took note of his sword, a long straight blade still in its scabbard, waiting. His clothing was similar to the other men around them, but he wore a burgonet instead of a cabasset, and his right hand was protected with a steel gauntlet. His face was covered in a thick black beard. He had a funny smirk that Fymurip found annoying.

"My lady Catherine," the man said, bowing low. "I greet you. I am Hector de Onis, captain of your father's royal guard. If it please you, my lady, I and my men have been charged with escorting you to El Palacio de la Aljafería, where your father and mother eagerly await your return."

Catherine remained silent, though Fymurip could see on her face that she was working out a response. Finally, she said, "I do not wish to attend my father's court, Captain de Onis."

"I am afraid, Lady Catherine," Captain de Onis said, "that a refusal is not possible. I have strict orders to escort you back to your father's house... and you will agree to it willingly, or I am instructed to deliver you by force."

"I see," Catherine said. She looked from man to man, clearly measuring their ability to move swiftly to do de Onis's orders. "And you are to deliver me alive, yes?"

Captain de Onis nodded. "Of course, my lady."

"Good," she said. "Now!"

Catherine moved faster than Fymurip had ever seen before, and he had seen her move very quickly in the past. She kicked the shield of the man closest to her, then drew the blade of her sword across his arms. He yelped and fell back, giving her room to move forward and eliminate the threat of a crossbowman who was raising his arms to fire.

"Don't fire!" Captain de Onis shouted, as he drew his own sword and tried moving against Catherine. "Take her alive!"

Fymurip blocked de Onis's path, but the captain was a skilled swordsman. His blade was out quickly, and he parried Fymurip's attack with efficient moves. But the Tatar hadn't fought all those years in the slave pits to be thwarted by a mere captain. He parried de Onis's thrust. Deflected another, and then stabbed the man's arm with his khanjar. He could have gone for the throat, the kill, but he took his lead from Catherine, who was clearly not fighting to kill either. She moved swiftly from one guardsman to another, cutting arms and legs like ribbons, but doing little permanent damage.

Together, they parried, slashed, and blocked their way through the bulk of their assailants. Catherine seemed intent on marking each man with her sword, and she nearly did so. But their weight and numbers were too great. In time, even Fymurip could not block all the bodies coming at him.

He was tripped and knocked to the ground. Five men fell upon him quickly, seized his blades, and held his arms behind his back. Fymurip could barely breathe, but he was thankful that Catherine was being treated more gently.

"If we had no intention of causing death," Fymurip said through the pressure of a heavy knee on his face, "why did we attack?"

Catherine grunted against their efforts to tie her hands together. "My father has to know that there is a cost in dealing with me."

"Wonderful," Fymurip said as his hands were being tied. "I'm sure he'll be most impressed with your skills with a blade. They may even take out their impression on an old Tatar soldier when we reach El Palacio whatever."

"They will not harm you," she said. "My mother is a kind woman. She will—"

"No more talk!" Captain de Onis said.

They were lifted up, and the captain stepped forward, wincing at the wound that Fymurip had delivered to his arm. "You are a skilled swordsman, Fymurip Azat. I look forward to finishing this engagement with you some day. But one thing more. Where is Tizona?"

Fymurip shook his head. "What are you talking about?"

De Onis cracked him across the face with a hard, solid hand. Fymurip gritted his teeth against the blow and felt blood trickle down his mouth. He spit. "I don't know what you are talking about."

De Onis was about to deliver a fresh one, when Catherine blurted, "By the fire. It sits by the fire."

They turned and looked towards the dying fire.

But Tizona and Alfredo were gone.

11

II

It was called the Palacio de la Aljafería, and Fymurip was glad that they had finally arrived, despite his wrists being numb from the cords that Captain de Onis's men had wrapped around them. He was glad because finally, at long last, Catherine paused in her constant beratement of his trust in Alfredo. When the mighty fortress came into view, she took time to gaze upon her childhood home. Fymurip reveled in it as well. It was a marvelous structure, rising out of a ring of Black Alder trees like a monument to the gods. It was worthy of anyone's respect. But the sweet view and calming silence did not last long.

"I told you not to trust the little monster," Catherine said as they were escorted on horseback across the stone bridge that connected the palace to a low wall and common walkway. "Didn't I tell you not to trust him?"

"You did," Fymurip said, as he had answered many times over the past few days. She never seemed to tire of asking it.

"Next time I tell you something about my country, about Spanish creatures and folklore, perhaps you'll listen."

On many occasions, he had wanted to snap back, to defend himself against her wrath, but in truth, Fymurip realized that he may have indeed made a terrible mistake. The little monster was gone, and so too, Tizona, quite likely never to be seen again. And it was his fault. Well, partially his fault at least. One man could never be blamed for every nefarious action perpetrated by a supernatural being. On one level or another, they were all tricksters and charlatans at heart. Their very nature demanded such. But he could have been more careful. When de Onis and his men arrived, he could have stepped back to the sword, stood over it to defend it. Now it was gone. Was their mission over? Fymurip did not know. Catherine certainly acted like it was. Despite her outward rage, he could see that inside, she was sad, depressed, though he didn't know if that was because of the loss of the sword, or the fact that she was about to see her royal parents again. Both, probably.

They were removed from their horses and their bonds cut. Fymurip breathed relief and rubbed his wrists until he could feel his hands again. Catherine did the same. They stood there and waited for the gate to be opened.

The side of the palace that they were on was guarded by six stone towers that held the wall together like a row of powerful teeth. Any enemy army, even one equipped with cannon, handgun, and trebuchet, would be foolish to face this side of the fortress without support from ten thousand men, or more. From their approach, Fymurip could not ascertain the might of the rest of the structure, but he figured it was formidable all the way around, and he could not wait to see the inside of it. For a moment, he felt guilty feeling such pleasure with his surrounds, and it was clear that Catherine certainly did not understand why he had such a pleasant glow on his face, especially after their capture. She glared at him in the same manner that she had done often in the past several days. Fymurip stowed his excitement.

"This way," Captain de Onis said, pushing a fist into Fymurip's back and pointing towards the gate, which was now raised to permit entry.

One of the men tried to handle Catherine in similar fashion. She kicked him in the shin, and he fell away holding his sore leg. "Back off! This is my home, and you will not touch me."

The man looked as if he were going to protest, but Captain de Onis waved him off.

As they walked through the gate and into the palace, Fymurip suddenly remembered that he did not have his sword and dagger with him. Catherine was without her weapon as well. They had been taken during the trip and not returned. Sound decision, Fymurip thought, and if he had been in charge, he'd have done the same thing. But as always, he felt naked without his blades. They had become such an important part of his life that the thought of being without them was almost hateful. Would he ever see them again? He did not know. Possibly, if he ever left the castle. Being Muslim, and so soon after the Reconquista, freedom was suspect, and suddenly Fymuip's revel in the majesty of the Aljafería was gone.

Waiting for them was Catherine's mother, the Queen Regent of Castile and Leon, Isabella I of the House of Trastamara.

*****

Despite all that had happened, despite all that Catherine had been through, had seen, the sight of her mother always made her feel small. She bowed immediately and gave Fymurip an elbow to do the same.

"Mother," Catherine said, bowing low. "It is nice to see you again."

"Rise, child," said the queen, holding out her hands to her daughter. Catherine took them. "You do not have to bow to me. I may be queen of Spain, but I am still just your mother."

They kissed cheeks, and Catherine could smell the sweet fragrance of the latest perfume that her mother always liked to splash on in the morning. The scent of it on the air stoked memories both pleasant and uncomfortable.

"Let me look at you," Isabella said, pulling away but still holding Catherine's hands. "My, have you grown."

Her mother had always been a short, stocky woman, but always in relative good health. Her hair now seemed a little darker than Catherine remembered it. She remembered a reddish blonde, leaning towards auburn. Today, it was near brown, with a few streaks of gray. That was understandable, Catherine figured. Having the responsibility of all of Spain - now that it was united under her and Father's banner - it was a wonder that her hair wasn't all gray. But her face was the same. That had not changed much, despite a few more wrinkles around the eyes. How old was Mother now? Catherine wondered. In her late forties, early fifties? The past few years had been a blur, and she had lost count. Catherine resembled her mother the most of any of her siblings. It was like looking into a mirror. Is this how I will look in thirty years?

The queen's clothing was more modest than Catherine would have imagined. It was a red-and-gold dress, with far less hoops than more traditional court costumery. The bodice was loose, and Catherine could see that her mother had put on a few pounds. That was understandable too, giving birth to so many children. She wore modest gold-colored slippers.

"Who is this?" Isabella asked, turning towards Fymurip.

"This is Fymurip Azat," Catherine said. "My travel companion. And I will say it now to spare time: he is Muslim, and he is not to be harmed while we are here."

Isabella looked at Catherine as if the words had stung. "Do you take me for cruel, my daughter? Or your father? The war is over.

The Reconquista concluded many years ago. I see no reason for harm at all. So long as he comports himself well while in my presence, he will be treated with the utmost respect and courtesy. Do you agree to those terms, Senor Azat?"

Fymurip nodded. *Si, su Majestad.*

Isabella's face beamed. "Ah, you speak Espanol."

Fymurip raised his left hand and showed his fingers as if he held something small between thumb and forefinger. "Un poco, your Grace. Catherine has been teaching me."

"I see. And has she also been teaching you the wonders of the Christian faith?"

"Mother…"

"There are many faiths, your Grace," Fymurip said, "and many gods. I choose to worship Allah, as you choose to worship God and his son, Christ Jesus. Many in the Slavic lands that Catherine and I have travelled worship Dazbog and Perun. In many respects, they are all one and the same."

Catherine reflexively reached for her sword that wasn't there. Fymurip was being quite bold, too bold perhaps, in his first meeting with the queen. She changed the subject quickly.

"Why have we been brought here, Mother?" she asked. "We are on a mission for the Hanseatic League. We can broach no delay."

"Catherine." Isabella rolled her eyes, and Catherine remembered her mother doing so when she was very little, right before she was about to condescend. "You are too young to be traipsing about Europe for those godless merchants. There is no need for that anymore. You are home, and you have responsibilities to your country and to your family."

"Where is Joanna?" Catherine said.

Isabella nodded. "She is here, as is your father. He wishes to speak with you immediately." She shot a glance at Fymurip. "Alone."

Tell him nothing. "I demand that you release us, Mother. You have no right."

"Catherine!" Isabella shouted, then quickly regained her composure. She smiled, shot glances at the battery of assistants, guards, and ladies-in-waiting that stood nearby. She took Catherine's hands once more. "Please, do not make a scene. Can I not have a few days of peace with my own daughter? Let us not have this argument today. Go, go and see your father. He is most anxious to see you again."

There was nothing more that Catherine could do. Without their swords, they could do very little, but try to run. And given the number of guards still in attendance, they would not get far. They were trapped, and they'd have to find a way to escape later.

Catherine breathed deeply to calm herself, nodded, and said, "Very well, Mother. What does Father wish to see me about?"

"Everything," Isabella said. "Everything. And especially, your pending marriage to Arthur."

III

They were separated. Father had been to see her father, King Ferdinand, and I want to take... to the room that he would stay in while
in attendance. He didn't like it. Not the room, it was adequate, but
being separated from... there he was troubling. Not that he didn't expect it. But the last time he had been separated from her... had come...
motion. Trumip had nearly been killed by a bright fight between
a jinn and an efreet. In effect, he did not expect to see either of those types
of creatures here, but this was a Moorish palace or... had been in its
day. Who knew what still might life in secret in the crevasses of dark
places. Superstitious creatures were eager that way, and they got
according themselves to the likudakites of mortals. Hyrum made
sure to check every conceivable place in his room that could contain
a trap, physical or otherwise.

"The Queen has granted you permission to walk the grounds
as you please," the guardsaid, who delivered Trumib to his room.
"But you will be escorted there by guard, and you will not be permitted to enter places that Her Highness deems sacred. Do you understand?"

The guard's speech was clipped and fast, but Hyrum was able
to pick out the relevant points: no missteps, grounds, guards, hear-
ings. That last point had not been uttered by the guard, but Trumib
knew that the warning lay below the words. Obtain the wrong place,
o Muslim, and you will be hunted.

Hyrum nodded. "Gratida."

He was left alone without an open window, fresh linens on his
uncluttered bed, a bowl of water and two large thin cloths, a sack of dry
tea, dumbling, and a half loaf of bread, the trace of a piece immediately.
and ate it with one bite, deciding its helpful, and at it. He took half
the water with one gulp. Then he sat down on the bed, ran his hands
across the soft sheets, closed his eyes, and sighed.

A long journey, and a hard fight. And now here he was, a
prisoner in the King of Spain's palace, and this was not how he had
planned it. It was not how Catherine had imagined it: he was not in
chains. And where was Trumip, who had little here? Already he was
gone, as usual.

III

They were separated, Catherine taken to see her father, King Ferdinand, and Fymurip taken to the room that he would stay in while in attendance. He didn't like it. Not the room. It was adequate. But being separated from Catherine was troubling. Not that he didn't expect it. But the last time he had been separated from his travel companion, Fymurip had nearly been killed by a brutal fight between a jinn and an efreet. He did not expect to see either of those types of creatures here, but this was a Moorish palace, or, had been in its day. Who knew what still might lie in secret in the crevasses of dark places? Supernatural creatures were cagey that way, and they did not confine themselves to the timetables of mortals. Fymurip made sure to check every conceivable place in his room that could contain a trap, physical or ethereal.

"The queen has granted you permission to walk the grounds as you please," the guard said who delivered Fymurip to his room. "But you will be escorted there by guard, and you will not be permitted to enter places that Her Highness deems sacred. Do you understand?"

The guard's Spanish was crisp and fast, but Fymurip was able to pick out the relevant points: permission, grounds, guards, beatings. That last point had not been uttered by the guard, but Fymurip knew that the warning lay below the words. Go into the wrong places, Muslim, and you will be beaten.

Fymurip nodded. *Entiendo.*

He was left alone with an open window, fresh linens on his modest bed, a bowl of water and two lavender cloths, a vase of water for drinking, and a half loaf of bread. He tore off a piece immediately and ate it with one bite, despite its being dry and stale. He took half the water with one gulp. Then he sat down on the bed, ran his hands across the soft sheets, closed his eyes, and sighed.

A long journey, and a long fight. And now here he was, a prisoner in the King of Spain's palace, and this was not how he had planned it. It was not how Catherine had imagined it, he was certain of that. And where was Tizona? And that little beast, Alfredo? Long gone, for sure.

He stood, tore off another piece of bread, but this time, he chewed slowly, savoring the flavor, the texture. He walked to the window.

It was a sunny day, but a light breeze caught his sweaty face and made it tolerable. He needed a bath, and he was sure that, this time, he would not be pampered by slave girls like he had been in the care of the Sultan. That was fine, as far as Fymurip was concerned. The last thing he needed right now was stimulation. He needed a bath, for sure, but more importantly, he needed time alone. Time alone to figure out his next move, and one that should involve Catherine. But would it? The Queen mentioned that Catherine was to marry a fellow named Arthur, and if Fymurip remembered correctly, he was the Prince of Wales. If so, then what point would it be for Fymurip to linger here, in this place, for longer than needed? Surely the King and Queen would release him once that matter was resolved. Fymurip chuckled. If Catherine had anything to say about it, the matter would be resolved with a knife across young Arthur's windpipe. How could he even think that Catherine would go along with the marriage? She'd sooner be dead than to submit to such an event.

Gaahh! Fymurip pulled off his tattered shirt and threw it into the corner. So many questions, unresolved, rolling through his mind. He didn't know what to do.

So, he ate bread and cleaned himself with the bowl of water and the lavender cloths. He soaked the cloths in the water, and then ran them across his arms, his chest, his shoulders, and sore neck. It felt good to clean away the grime on his neck. On his face too, and he lingered with the wet cloth around his eyes and forehead and scrubbed them till they were red and raw. He ran a cloth across his head as well, letting his dry hair soften and fluff in the water. It all felt wonderful.

Now his body was clean. His soul needed cleansing as well.

Was there a mosque on the grounds? Fymurip wondered. The Palacio de la Aljafería had been a Moorish palace before the Reconquista, and so there must be some structure on the grounds that had once served as its mosque. Probably not anymore, though. If the building still remained at all. It could very well have been demolished as a symbol of the eradication of Islam in Europe. But Fymurip needed to pray. It had been a long time since he had done so. Prayer always helped him sort out his thoughts and reveal hidden feelings.

He made a note to inquire about it later and went to pick up his shirt. Then he heard her voice.

It was a beautiful, lilting voice on the breeze, emanating from the palace courtyard just below his window. He dropped his shirt and went to see.

There she was, a young lady, her back to him, her light red hair radiant in the sun. She picked flowers among a bed of red carnations and bluebells. She reached her delicate hand out and touched a rose, and then she leaned over to sniff it and enjoy its tender scent. Fymurip did not recognize the song she was singing, but to him, it sounded like an angel.

Then she turned. He saw her face and recognized it immediately.

"Catherine?"

*****

Catherine was escorted to the north side of the grounds, where construction had been ordered to create a main hall and throne room so the current (and future) Catholic kings and queens of Spain could conduct their business, outside of the older Islamic areas of the palace. The work was unfinished, but the throne room was in place and functional. A little stark, for sure, but it served the purposes of her royal father, who sat atop his royal throne, waiting.

Isabella bid her daughter goodbye by kissing her hand, without a word, and then left swiftly through a side door, followed by her doting entourage.

Ferdinand II of Aragon, King of Spain, was a soft man. Now, in his fifties, the warm roll of his face accentuated his small chin. His eyes were large and perhaps his best feature; open, alert, and gentle. He still had his hair, which was dark and thick. At present, it was pushed underneath a black felt bonnet, and he wore golden layers of clothing to represent his house. Like her mother, the King's clothing was more relaxed, just a tunic and light half coat. He wore black stockings and slippers. He did not smile, though his face was bright, and perhaps belied his attempt as seeming stern and authoritarian in the presence of his doting entourage.

"Father," Catherine said with a little curtsy. "It is nice to see you again."

The King did not respond immediately. He let her salutation linger there, in the air, and let her suffer a moment. Then he whispered quietly so that Catherine could barely hear it. "You do not seem sincere."

"It is as sincere as I can make it, my Lord. I do not know what more to say."

Ferdinand stood. He wasn't a short man, but he wasn't tall either. Just plain. He walked to her and extended his hand as if he expected her to kiss it. Catherine bowed her head, but dared not lay lips on that wrinkled hand. Nor his sigil ring.

Ferdinand put his hand down, quickly. "You have given your mother nothing but grief, my daughter. She has worried about you sunrise to sunset."

"There was no reason to worry," she said, lifting her head to speak more clearly. "I sent word whenever I could."

"Yes, through couriers of the Hanseatic League. But I do not understand why a girl, and one so young as you, would dare to associate with that merchants' guild. You have never expressed an interest in mercantile matters your entire life, and yet you traipse around all of Europe doing their bidding. Why?"

"The Hanseatic League does more than trade, Father," Catherine said, following the King to the window behind his throne. "You know this."

"What I know is that they deal in heresy, and by associating yourself with them, you do as well." Ferdinand turned to his daughter, his face no longer soft, but drawn and serious, his eyes wide. "Dealing with the supernatural, fighting creatures of shadow, mingling with Slavic Gods and Eldar Gods, and who knows what else. Unholy nonsense!"

Catherine tried to avoid chuckling, but she let slip a tiny laugh. "Something cannot be nonsense, Father, and also be considered unholy. Either one or the other, but not both."

"Do you mock me, my daughter?"

"My name is Catherine."

"And who do you think named you?"

Catherine backed off a pace as her father's guard came closer. A deathly silence fell between them. Ferdinand turned to the window and stared out onto his courtyard. Catherine gave him space, for despite her desire to win this argument, it was folly to fight the King in his own throne room. She could not win a shouting match.

Not here.

She curtsied again, though he did not see it. "Forgive me, Father. I did not wish to offend. But my work with the League is important, not only for the world, but for Spain as well. The Eldar Gods are real, Father, and they do not care about political borders, or whether you or Mother worship the one and only God. Someday, they will come to Spain, and the armies that you wielded so successfully at Grenada will not be enough if but one Eldar God enters the world unfettered. I implore you, Father. Accept the deal that I offered you when I left. Let me be your eyes and ears of the world. And I promise you, together - you, me, and Mother - can protect Spain from something far more deadly than a Muslim Caliphate."

Ferdinand lingered there at the window, as if he were truly considering her offer. And perhaps he was. It was difficult to know. Then he turned to her, a tiny smile on his small mouth, and said, "Do not worry about Spain, Catherine. I have Diego de Deza and the Inquisition to keep us safe."

Catherine huffed. "They waste time expelling and killing Jews and false heretics. And now you know why I left Spain."

Ferdinand waved his hand. "This discussion is over. I wish to hear no more. It hardly matters anyway, for you are home now, and you will stay and do your duty to me, your mother, and to Spain. The Prince of Wales is scheduled to arrive within four days. The marriage will take place shortly thereafter."

Catherine shook her head ferociously. "I will not marry Arthur. I will not."

"Alliances are what matters, Catherine," Ferdinand said. "Alliances are what will protect us from whatever is out there in the wide world." He nodded to his guards. "Please show my daughter Catherine to her quarters."

A guard moved to take her arm. She smacked his hand away. "Don't touch me. I will see myself out."

The guard looked at his king, and Ferdinand shook his head, sighed, and nodded. "Let her go."

Catherine turned and stomped out.

What a fool! Why did I ever bother coming back to Spain? Cowards... all of them!

She needed air, fresh air. She needed food, something to drink, and a bath. She needed a Mother and Father who could look beyond the veiled promises of a God that they believed in but could never see. She needed a kind shoulder to rest her weary head upon. She needed to get as far away as she could before the Prince of Wales arrived. She needed a lot of things.

But first, air. She walked down the hallway and towards the light that would lead her to the courtyard.

IV

"**C**atherine?"

Fymurip stepped out into the courtyard, into the hot sun that radiated heat off the beautiful stone walkway. A guard followed closely but did not try to impede his approach to the young woman. She seemed to be oblivious to his presence.

"Catherine?" he said again as he came up to her.

She turned, smiled.

Fymurip bowed. "Forgive me, miss. I thought you were -"

"Catherine, my sister," she said, a wry smile on her beautiful red lips. She passed a tongue through those lips, letting the tip linger there before speaking further. "A lot of people make that mistake, for we look so alike, so much like our mother. But no, I am Joanna, or, as the wonderful common folk call me, *Juana la Loca*. But I'm not crazy. In this world, there is indeed a fine line between ecstatic vision and insanity. But I'm not crazy, I assure you. Do you think I'm crazy?"

Her expression was so sincere, Fymurip took her words seriously. "No, my lady, I... I don't know you well enough to say."

She laughed, a high-pitched lilt that sent a sparrow nearby to wing. Joanna watched as the bird flew out of the courtyard and into the light of the warm sun. "You know who I am. Now you... wait! I know who you are. You are... Fymurip Azat," she said, squinting in the light as if she were pulling his name out of her mind with pincers. "Is that your name?"

He nodded. "Yes, my lady."

She approached him, closer than he felt comfortable, but the flowery scent off her damp skin locked him in place. She smiled. "The famous Fymurip Azat, braving the countryside of Spain on a grand adventure with Catherine of Aragon. How exciting."

"Well," he said, clearing his throat, "I don't know how exciting it is, my lady. Dangerous, yes, but exciting..."

She touched his arm, ran her fingers down his skin to his hand. Fymurip froze, then relaxed. Her voice was very soothing.

"Don't be modest, now. I know all about you. I know about you and Catherine's journey. You are here to find Tizona, are you not?" She leaned in and whispered, "And tell me, did you find it?"

What should he say? How much did she really know? She could be bluffing, he knew, throwing out questions based on rumor and whispers between de Onis's guardsmen. She could be a trickster, taking human form to lure Fymurip into a confession, and then use that confession against him, against his mortal soul. But she seemed real enough, and all the supernatural creatures that he had ever come in contact with never smelled so sweet, nor smiled, so sincerely. "We lost it," he confessed.

Joanna's expression turned sad, her bottom lip protruding in sorrow. "Ah, that is too bad. For the dragon must not rise, eh?"

"What?"

She ignored his question. Instead, she winked at him and then returned to her flowers. "Come, keep me company. You are such an interesting man."

So, Fymurip kept Joanna the Mad company as she moved from flowerbed to flowerbed, smelling, touching, and identifying to him all the different flowers in abundance in the Courtyard of Santa Isabel: poppies and bluebells, roses and red carnations, lantanas and gazanias, and so many others that Fymurip lost count and interest. They looked wonderful; they smelled, like her, even better. But the sun was hot, and the bed was calling. He felt like he was walking in his sleep.

"Some mistakenly assume the courtyard was named after my mother, with the name of Isabella and all, but that is not true. This place was named after the infanta Elizabeth of Aragon, many centuries ago. Some said she was a saint, like my mother, but I remember her as a bitch."

Fymurip was pulled from his dream state. "What... how, how, my lady, could you have..."

Joanna cuddled up beside him, wrapping her arm around his. She giggled. "I'm joking... joking. How could I possibly be that old and stay so beautiful? You do think me beautiful, don't you?"

Joanna halted, turned into Fymurip's path and held both his hands. "Do you think I'm beautiful?"

"Yes, my lady." Fymurip said the words before he knew what he had said. But they were his words, not coerced from any mesmerism that he could sense in the air, nor any trickery on her part. Her eyes, her breath, her smile… all hers. "I think you are most beautiful."

Concern shadowed Joanna's face. She squeezed his hands. "Look at you… falling asleep with every word I utter. That will not do. Come with me, to my chamber, and I will help you sleep."

She pulled his arm. Fymurip baulked. "My lady, I… but where is your husband? Do you not have a husband?"

Joanna's face beamed. "Oh, yes, and the most beautiful man in all the world. *Philip the Handsome* he is called. And what a wonderful lover, too. I am blessed. But he would not care if you came to my room. He is surely in some silly girl's bed right now anyway. So come, and I will take care of you."

He wanted to say no. But she was so soft, her words so pleasant, and he was so, so tired. Her smile was beautiful, her hair so red. She looked so much like Catherine…

"Yes, all right," he said, letting her guide him forward.

She giggled. "Oh, wonderful. You will not regret this decision. You will—"

"JOANNA!"

*****

Fymurip jumped as Catherine's shout echoed across the courtyard. "Let him alone, Joanna."

Joanna stopped. Her glee turned to annoyance, anger, as she too seemed startled by her sister's command. Then her expression softened to buoyancy, as she flung herself onto Catherine and gave her a powerful squeeze. "My sister Catherine. It is so good to see you. I prayed every night for your return."

Catherine did not hug back, though she did pat Joanna on the back and rolled her eyes for Fymurip to see. She did not say anything, waiting perhaps, for Joanna to continue, so as to avoid being interrupted. Joanna did not disappoint.

"Please, you must tell me everything," Joanna said, taking her sister's arms. "Everything."

"Some other time, perhaps," Catherine said. "And don't change the subject. I know what you were about to do."

"And what was that?" Joanna asked, turning to look at Fymurip. Both sisters were looking at him now. "To help him sleep? To place his head on a pillow, and make him feel like a man again?"

"Joanna..."

"Oh, all right. I relent. You may have him back. But take care of him, Catherine." Joanna winked at Fymurip. "Do not try to turn him into a scholar, into a man of thought and heavy contemplation. Do not try to turn him into the second coming of Ibn Battuta. Fymurip Azat is a man of action, of danger. And you will need his sword before the end. Both of them. All three."

Joanna giggled. Catherine pushed her sister away and made to shoo her as if she were a fly. "Go, *Juana la Loca*. Go and smell your roses. We will talk later."

Joann nodded. "Yes, we will. For I need to know everything. If I am to one day rule this land, I need to know it all. And you, my fair, frigid sister, must remember: *El dragon no puede levantarse*."

Catherine did not respond. Instead, she merely nodded at those last words, and then waited until Joanna slowly bid Fymurip goodbye with a tender kiss on his cheek, and then drifted away into song and further beds of flowers.

When she was far out of earshot, Catherine took Fymurip's hand and said, "Come, let's get a bath."

Fymurip baulked. "A bath? Together?"

Catherine pulled him along. "Yes."

V

V

Catherine led Fymurip through the palace and into the so-called Taifal section, which comprised a part of Aljafaria named after the once-grand Taifa city-state of Zaragoza. Many, many years ago. As they entered the bath house, Fymurip read an Arabic inscription that had not been removed from the walls by the current occupants:

Oh Palace of the Joy! Oh Golden Hall!
Because of you, I reached the maximum of my wishes.
And even though in my kingdom I had nothing else,
for me you are everything I could wish for.

They were lovely words, and for a moment, Fymurip wished he were in his home country, or anywhere in the Middle East for that matter. He missed his people.

"Is there a mosque here?" Fymurip asked as they prepared to bathe. "Somewhere I can be alone for a time?"

Catherine nodded and pointed towards the Golden Hall that they had passed through. "Somewhere over there. You can find it."

She began to remove her clothing, and Fymurip turned quickly to keep from seeing her. "What is the matter? Have you never seen a naked woman?"

Fymurip nodded. "Yes, but... never one so young."

"Don't worry," she said. "We are not going to do what Joanna had in mind for you. We are just going to bathe. I need a bath. I need to calm down a little. And we need to talk. That is all."

Fymurip calmed by settling down in the warm water, making sure that he was appropriately far enough away from Catherine as to be acceptable to anyone who might find them there. She did the same, and so they took a few minutes to relax and wash away the grime of the road, the grime of the world. Fymurip felt like dozing, but he forced himself to stay awake and keep his eyes on Catherine. Not to look at her nakedness, no, but react to anything she might do or say while they were here, together and alone.

Catherine spoke first. "My father has ordered me to marry Prince Arthur of Wales."

She paused, and Fymurip could see the anger and fear on her face. "Are you going to?"

"I want to get married someday," she said, "but not now, and certainly not to Arthur, whom' we know in the Hanseatic League is rumored to have affiliations with dark forces. Which forces I do not know - perhaps Eldar. I have never been tasked to find out."

Fymurip shrugged. "Perhaps marrying him will bring you into contact with those forces. Then you'll be in a position to fight them, destroy them."

Catherine paused and seemed as if she were considering the idea. "Or be corrupted just like him. No," she said, moving a little to the left, waving her arms to splash warm water on her face, "it would be foolish for me to marry just for that, to be near a man just to, one day, wind up killing him. A lot of good people are corrupted by the Eldar gods, Fymurip. Prince Arthur may very well be a good man, a nice man, but I won't marry him for that. Nor will I go through the same pain and struggle my mother did when she was young. I cannot tell you how many times my grandfather tried to force her into one marriage or another, all with an eye on securing alliances. My mother was strong enough to resist them all, until she finally settled on my father. They wore her down, Fymurip, and my mother settled. I refuse to settle. I want to marry someday, but I will choose who that person will be."

Catherine was staring right at him. Was it a sign? Was she indicating through that stare that he, Fymurip Azat, was the man she wanted to marry? The notion was too much for him to consider right now. "But look at your mother: she is one of the most powerful women in all of Europe, in all the world I'd say, because of her marriage."

"True but consider the circumstances. The Moors had been pushed back and back and back for centuries, until such a time as my mother and father assumed the throne. At that point, all it took was just another big push, and finally, Spain was theirs. Their rise to power was just as much luck and opportunity as anything else.

"And what will a marriage to Prince Arthur get me? A navy? A seat beside him on a throne in England? What advantage does that miserable little island get me? And besides, marrying Arthur would put me dangerously close to that sniveling little wretch of a brother, Henry. They say he fucks anything that moves. I do not wish to give him a new target."

Catherine speaking so frankly about marriage, about sex, made Fymurip uncomfortable. No woman in the Muslim world would dare speak like this in front of a man, though Fymurip always suspected that women confided in each other behind closed doors with such talk. He snickered inwardly. If Lux were here, the Teutonic knight would blame her frankness on the fact that she was royalty, and that they always say what they wanted regardless of setting. Unlike many of her station, Catherine had shown great resistance to her exalted status. Leaving home, working for the Hanseatic League, and becoming an assassin... well, those were things that boys, men, did, not girls, and especially royal girls like Catherine, who were expected to marry to either maintain or improve the status of their station.

He changed the subject. "Your sister, Joanna. Is she really mad?"

Catherine lay back in the water. She closed her eyes, chuckled. "They don't call her *Juana la Loca* for nothing. She has always been that way, for as long as I've been alive."

"Do you suspect that she has been compromised?"

"By the Eldar gods?" She shook her head. "I don't think so. I've been around enough people who were such that I can sense it. She does not reflect any aura of rage, anger... evil. She is mad, indeed, but it is borne more out of excessive amorous and lust than darkness. She has visions, though they are muddled and confused. I don't think even she understands them."

"And your parents do not know?"

"They know, but it hardly matters to them. Their precious Joanna will be queen someday, and thus she can never be seen as crazy, mad. If it were me in her place, Father would have already summoned the Inquisition."

Fymurip could tell that the mention of the Inquisition upset her. Her face turned angry, unsettled. He couldn't blame her for that. The stories he had heard about the Spanish Inquisition were legendary and fearful. "So, what do we do now?"

Catherine was silent for a long while. Then, she said, "We wait, for a time. The security of the castle is far too great, even for us, to try to run. Arthur is to arrive within four days, so we have time to consider our options."

"That isn't a lot of time, Catherine," Fymurip said, risking a move closer to her. He stopped about ten feet away from her. "Four days will pass quickly, and then what? Do we even still have a mission?"

Catherine fluffed her hair out, as if she were shaking it free from soil and bugs. Then she submerged herself completely and lingered there beneath the water for a full minute. Fymurip was about to grow concerned. Then she emerged, her hair all wet and smooth, clinging to the back of her head and down her shoulders. Fymurip was amazed at how different she looked with her hair all wet. He could see her face now clearly, and she was beautiful. So —

"I think we should go after Colada."

*****

Catherine could tell that her sudden change of heart startled her companion. "Really? I thought you said that would be foolish."

"No, I never said that. But then, we had Tizona, and yes, it would have been foolish for us to risk going after another sword. But Tizona is gone, and we have failed the League. I see no other option before us but to rectify the matter as best we can and go after Colada. That means going to Madrid and breaking into the Royal Alcazar... where my parents usually reside. They are here merely to ensure my marriage to Arthur. Now is the right time, for security there will be lax because my parents are not there. If we get Colada, we can ensure that, at least, one of El Cid's swords is secure."

It was Fymurip's time to duck under the water. He did so, and Catherine tried not to look as his body stretched out. She couldn't resist just a short peek.

He emerged, slicked his hair back like she had done. He did not speak, at least not right away. He was thinking. She had been around the man long enough to know when he was trying to plan, to plot, to work out a means of escape, but it did not appear that he had succeeded.

"All right," he said, "so how do we go?"

Catherine shook her head. "I don't know yet. Arthur may be here in four days, yes, but the wedding will take longer to prepare. My parents will want to make a big show of it, to announce to all the world that their youngest daughter will marry into the Tudor line. It will take another week, if not longer, to make sure the proper people are here in witness of the event. The Catholic Church must be involved as well. So, we have longer than four days, Fymurip. We have time to prepare."

She looked at her hand. She was wrinkling badly in the hot water. "I'm done," she said, and climbed out of the tub. And as she did, she hoped that Fymurip was watching. But the silly man was probably not, convinced, she supposed, that averting his eyes would be the proper thing to do. Foolish man! Look at me. Look at me.

She wrapped herself with a large white towel and rubbed her hair dry. She felt good, oh so good, now that all the dirt and sweat from the road was gone. Fymurip ended her euphoria with one simple question.

"Your sister talked about a dragon, and that it should not rise again. What did she mean by that?"

Catherine shrugged, trying desperately not to show worry or concern on her face. "Who can say? She's *Juana la Loca*, remember?"

"But she mentioned it before you appeared in the garden, and then once again before we left. It's as if she wanted you to hear it. What does it mean?"

"I don't know. Perhaps we'll find out in time," Catherine said, finishing off her hair and then redressing the towel wrapped around her so that it would not slip. "Get dressed and find something to eat. We will try to meet as often as we can — as often as they let us — to make plans. Now, I have to go and pretend to be the model daughter, and you must pretend to be the model guest."

She bowed politely to him, turned, grabbed up her clothing, and then fled through a side door.

He knows, she thought as she walked into another room to find privacy to dress. He knows I am holding back. He's too smart not to know. And again, why am I not telling him about the dragon? What harm could it do?

A lot of harm, Catherine believed, potentially at least. And none of it would matter anyway if they stole Colada and got away before her father, before his Inquisition, could be summoned to track them down. For that is what would surely happen if she and Fymurip ever escaped the palace, Catherine knew. Her father would never tolerate another deception, another escape.

So, for now, she would play the perfect daughter, as she had just told Fymurip. She would play the part, and it had always been the most difficult thing for her to do.

IV

VI

For the next four days, as they awaited the arrival of Prince Arthur, Fymurip kept his head down and tried to keep out of Princess Joanna's sight. It was difficult to do. She seemed to be everywhere, talking to everyone, and almost always in the garden, even when it rained. Was there more than one of her? Was she, through her madness, able to tap into energies that allowed her to be in different places at different times? Fymurip had never heard of anyone, any creature, doing such a thing, but he was learning more and more about the wide world every day, and he could not discount the possibility. But he did as Catherine bid: he played the model guest and kept out of her sister's path as best as possible.

Captain de Onis, surprisingly, allowed Fymurip to handle an arquebus. On one of his exploratory walks around the palace, Fymurip stumbled upon the king's guards practicing sword, archery, and gun work. He had never handled a pistol in his life, which, given all of his travels, was quite surprising. Perhaps he had always been a little afraid of it. It was different, something that he knew would change the course of warfare in the world forever. It was already beginning to do so. But in his line of work, an arquebus was too long, too loud, and took too long to prepare for firing, even one with a constantly burning match. It was never a good option for him in Starybogow. But now, he was offered to try it out. And so he did.

The one he was allowed to use was a little less than three feet long. It was heavier than he imagined, given the overall simplicity of its construction. It was really nothing more than a piece of wood for a stock and a long iron barrel. Where its complexity resided was in its matchlock system for ignition.

It had what de Onis called a serpentine match lock, which was shaped like a serpent's head, and it held a small length of smoldering match. The rest of the burning cord was wrapped around the stock, and de Onis told him that as the match burned, the coil was loosened so as to allow the burning end of it to be as close as possible to the "touch hole" at all times, which was where the fire would strike the powder charge, ignite, and propel the lead ball through the barrel.

"But be cautious," de Onis said, as he helped Fymurip take aim for his first shot. "You do not want to squeeze the trigger handle too quickly and accidentally fire before you are ready. Unless, of course, you wish to blow the head off the person next to you."

That brought a series of chuckles from the men who were observing. But despite de Onis's frivolity, Fymurip could see the seriousness of the situation in the man's eyes: an arquebus was a dangerous weapon, and not to be handled carelessly.

The handle trigger was the extension of the serpentine head that held the match. It was on the bottom side of the stock, and Fymurip was supposed to squeeze it against the stock once he was ready to fire. This would drive the serpent's head down and place its burning match into the touch hole, and God willing, light the powder.

Fymurip aimed and squeezed the trigger. He heard the initial sizzle of the powder and then a loud, concussive blast. His shoulder was nearly dislocated from the recoil.

A loud cheer went up among de Onis's men as Fymurip lay on the ground, clutching his shoulder, and gritting his teeth against the pain. De Onis helped him to his feet, ordered him to fire again, and again, and again, until Fymurip was striking the target consistently. By the end of an hour of training, he was skilled enough to know how tightly to hold the stock against this shoulder, how to aim the barrel straight, and how to compensate for the spin of the ball out of the muzzle. By the end of training, he had become quite skilled. De Onis was impressed. So much so that he patted Fymurip on the back and invited him to join the guard… if he chose to stay in Zaragoza after the wedding.

Fymurip nodded politely, smiled, but remained non-committal.

Training sent him once again to the bath house in order to soothe away the pain in his shoulder and arms. Firing a gun brought a whole new set of muscles to work. Fymurip was skilled at stabbing and slashing, but not holding his arms up for long lengths of time, aiming, and taking a strong recoil against his shoulder. His entire body ached. The warm water was soothing, and this time, he took a bath without Catherine.

He also found a mosque, off the eastern entrance to the Golden Hall. It was a small room, but more than appropriate for his needs. It was barren, and obviously had not been used for years, perhaps decades. There was no carpet on which to kneel in prayer, but Fymurip did the best he could. Despite the fact that it was the middle of the day and he had missed some prayers, he performed all the rataks in order— the Fajr, the Zuhr, the Asr—and all the others, as best he could, on aching knees.

In the four days prior to Prince Arthur's impending arrival, he only saw Catherine once.

*****

For her part, Catherine played the model daughter, or, at least, tried to. So much was roiling around in her mind, fighting for control of her attention—the mission for the League, her impending wedding, her relationship with her parents, her incorrigible sister, Fymurip Azat. All of these things fought for control of her time, and she barely slept as they waged war behind closed eyes. She kept to herself mostly, taking time to spend with her mother when necessary, allowing herself to be properly fitted for a wedding dress, being fawned over by ladies-in-waiting and all manner of body servants who would not even let her relieve herself in private. She actually began to resent Fymurip and his freedom to roam the castle as he pleased, with only a few restrictions. But then, he wasn't the one getting married, was he? He wasn't the one that they needed to keep an eye on. In fact, Catherine figured that if he wanted to, Fymurip could walk right out of the front gate and no one would stop him. But he wouldn't do that, not when they still had a mission to accomplish. Not while she was still here and in jeopardy of being married off so some foreign prince with questionable ties to darkness.

Would he?

Over the past couple days, she had tried, on more than one occasion, to meet with him, but always there were guards nearby, and most certainly, if they were to meet, her father would know about it. And that might put Fymurip's life, or his freedom at least, in jeopardy. She could not allow that to happen. Whatever happened to her, she would not allow him to be harmed in any way.

Did that mean she loved him? She had asked herself that question more than once on their journey through Spain. She had wanted to kiss him after the matter with Duke Frederick and the Eldar priest outside Starybogow, but she had declined to do so. Why? And in the bath house, the sight of him, his slender, well-muscled body beneath the water, had almost made her swoon. He was a bed of scars from head to toe, for sure, but scars that he had gotten in the service of something greater than himself. And so too was she in the service for the very same thing, and the emotions from that service were paramount right now. Yes, she would confess it to herself, she loved Fymurip Azat. But no one else could know of it for now. Now, there were more pressing matters to attend to, like trying to figure a way out of her marriage to the Prince of Wales.

The day of his impending arrival came and went, and no prince arrived. The fifth day fell away, and still no prince. Catherine was beginning to hope that perhaps he had changed his mind. It was unheard of, really, for a prince to come to his betrothed. More often it went the other way, with the burden of travel laid at the feet of the girl. But the king and queen of Spain were powerful enough to demand the prince attend them at their own castle. And so they waited, and waited, and Catherine rejoiced.

The sixth day came, and finally, Prince Arthur arrived.

VII

Arthur Tudor, he the Prince of Wales, the Earl of Chester, and the Duke of Cornwall, arrived in Zaragoza to all the fanfare entitled one of royal blood and a future son-in-law of the Spanish Crown, though Catherine remembered larger, more ceremonious events in the past, such as when Pope Alexander VI paid a visit at the beginning of his reign in 1492. For his part, Arthur brought with him only a few body servants and one counselor, figuring perhaps that his stay would be brief, so why bear the expense? He was greeted warmly by the king and queen and their court, and then given an early afternoon feast with dancers, musicians, jugglers, and various other entertainers that provided some relief to Catherine's disdain and fear. She could, at least, enjoy the festivities while she tried to figure a way out of this mess. Things were moving faster for her than she had planned, but she endured all the food and wine and merriment as a dutiful daughter of Spain should.

Then the party ended, and she and Prince Arthur were given a moment alone so that they might get to know one another before the blessed event. The prince offered up a letter to Catherine and thanked her for her pleasant invitation so Spain.

Arthur was not an ugly boy. Quite the contrary. With his soft, red hair and his small, dark, comely eyes, Catherine felt surprisingly comfortable in his presence. And if their first face-to-face meeting had stayed simple and pleasant and unblemished by matters of state, things might have turned out differently, at least in the short term. As it was, even Arthur's tall and confident stature wasn't enough to keep Catherine from growing annoyed as their private meeting progressed.

She gripped the letter that Prince Arthur had given her. She held it out before her, pointing its crumpled corners at the prince like a dagger. She spoke to him in Latin because that's what learned royalty was supposed to do; plus, she didn't understand English as well as she might. Her duties to the Hanseatic League hadn't given her the opportunity to speak a lot of English. Her Latin was accurate, though a little muddled.

"I did not write this letter, my prince, and with respect, I did not invite you to my family's court, to Spain, or to anywhere."

Arthur seemed nonplussed by her admission. He even smiled a little. "I know that we were supposed to meet in England," Arthur said. "That would have been most ideal, but sometimes fate dictates a person's path." He pointed to the letter. "That letter is what compelled me to come. It was sealed in wax with your family's royal crest, my lady, and signed by your own hand."

Catherine shook her head. "A forgery, for you see, the date would make it impossible for me to have written this letter. I was in Prussia at the time, and -"

Arthur waved his delicate, perfumed hand to cut her off. "Please, fair Catherine, let us not quibble about these kinds of details. Whether you wrote the letter or not, I have responded to your - to the - invitation for us to marry here, in Spain, and if the gods are kind, that is exactly what I intend to do... per our royal obligations to our countries and the needs of our families."

"Gods? There is only one god, my prince."

Catherine lowered the letter and watched Arthur's face carefully, waiting to see if anything, a smirk or a frown, might pass across it to reveal what she and the League and so many others already suspected: The Prince Arthur was in league with the Eldar Gods. Nothing. Arthur's expression did not change. His face was unmarred by rage or confusion. It was beautiful. Too beautiful, in fact.

Catherine calmed herself by putting on her most excellent smile. "You're right. There is no reason to argue over a silly letter. You are here, and if the gods are kind, as you say, our wedding will go forward. Are the gods kind, Prince Arthur? Have they ever been kind to you?"

Arthur seemed to miss the question. He did not respond to it. Instead, he took two glasses of red wine from his body servant, offered one up to Catherine, and waited until the man hurried away. Arthur then offered a toast. "To our grand union, fair Catherine. May we live long. May our houses reign supreme. And may our children inherit the Earth."

The thought of having children with this boy, despite his beauty, made Catherine's stomach turn. She took a sip of wine and tried bringing the matter to a close, or to a head. "May our children inherit the Earth? My, Prince Arthur, you have lofty goals."

He nodded and finished his wine with a long drink. "It should be the goal of every father to see his children succeed, and exceed, him."

"But even if our children do inherit the Earth, as you say, England is only one small island. Not even as large as my Spain. How can two moderately-sized kingdoms hope to inherit the Earth?"

"Together," Prince Arthur said, a lilt rising in his voice as his expression grew stern, his eyes darker, "England and Spain can defeat any and all enemies that they face. Especially France. Together, we can bring that petty little country to heel and make it bleed."

Catherine put on her most surprised expression. "Is it war, then, my prince? Our bedsheets will hardly be soiled before you'll be fitting on your armor to lead men to battle. I had no idea you were so... militant."

Arthur smiled. "My family thinks me sickly, but I tell you that I am not. And I am far more qualified to rule than my sniveling little brother Henry. Anything we can do to keep that cretin off the throne is worth doing. And bringing France to its knees is icing on the cake and will ensure my rule for decades to come. We can achieve this, my bride, so long as I have a strong woman at my side. And I hear you have strength."

Well, Catherine agreed with him on two of those points: Indeed, Henry should never sit the throne of England, and yes, she was a strong woman. But would she be giving up that strength if she cowed to political pressure and gave herself to this boy. This boy who was, to her surprise, a more confident and stable soul than she had been led to believe.

Still, she needed proof. "What you say excites me, my prince. Spain is no lover of France, indeed, but to crush them. So many innocent people would die in such a powerful stroke."

"Then let them die!"

There it was. Arthur's expression turned from confidence to ecstatic, dark vision. "The French have never conceded to show us mercy. Why should we ever show it to them? They are meaningless in our quest for perfection. But, let us not worry ourselves today about our ultimate goals, fair Catherine. Let us join our hands, and prey, our lips, to confirm this union and to confirm our commitment to marry in a few short days."

He leaned in, and it was almost comical the way his thin lips puckered, the way his eyes closed. Like a child kissing his first girl.

And perhaps that's exactly what this was. Prince Arthur was young, just like she.

She leaned in too, though she kept her eyes open. She did not want to do this, to kiss this boy, to listen anymore to his militant, hateful rhetoric. In her heart, Catherine did not like France any more than he did, but to bury them in war, in death, and in desolation as he seemed to be suggesting was too much.

Kiss him, and be done with it, she told herself.

She pressed her lips to his, and everything she had suspected of this young man came to light. Perhaps his guard was down, perhaps his youth, coupled with being alone in a room with a girl that he would soon marry, had brought down the barrier between the visage that he shared with the world and the one he showed the Eldar Gods. Whatever the reason, Prince Arthur's soul lay bare to her in that kiss, and Catherine saw a vision of the future that terrified her. There would indeed be no more France, if Arthur's plans came to fruition. There would be no Spain either, no Europe at all. And all the world would lay in fire and ash.

Catherine forced herself to not scream out in fear. She pulled away from the kiss, smiled as best she could, curtsied politely as a good, Christian princess should do, then bid the pleasant prince good night.

Before she was clear of the door, the tears coursed down her face.

*****

The next morning, she found her sister in the courtyard. "Joanna, you must help me."

Joanna seemed not to notice her at first, so enraptured in song and butterflies. Then she turned, a bright red, long-stem poppy in her hand, the petals held against her face. "My sweet sister. Good morning."

"No, it is a dark morning," Catherine said. "Arthur has arrived."

"Yes, I am aware. I was at the feast, remember? It's going to be a glorious wedding, is it not? He's a handsome boy, no?"

Catherine shook her head. "I don't care about how he looks. I need you to help me convince Father and Mother that the wedding should not occur. I'm to meet with him again in two hours." She huffed and rolled her eyes in disgust. "To be presented to him officially as if I'm property."

Joanna reached out with a delicate hand and touched Catherine's shaking arm. "But you are, my sister. You are property. At least in the eyes of your father king. All daughters are property in this world. Have you been away so long that you do not remember what is expected of us?"

Catherine patted away Joanna's hand and stepped closer. She had to control herself and not reach for the dagger tied to her thigh, the one neither her parents nor the guards knew about. "Don't play me for a fool, or naive, sweet sister. I am well aware of my station in the eyes of our father. You speak as if you understand, and practice, such submission yourself, though I know for a fact that you sleep with as many men as your handsome husband sleeps with women. You do not play the role of the 'obedient wife'. In Spain, your husband is allowed such frivolity, Juana la Loca... but not you."

Joanna's expression and mood changed, as if hearing the term that she was called in whispers around court affected her deeply. She forced a smile. "You have always been too open and free with your objections to how things are, Catherine. You see the world too plainly, perhaps, and react to it in the same manner. But not all of us were gifted with your physical skills, your incessant drive for self-determination. The rest of us must use the tools we have. So if my... frivolity, as you call it... is incompatible with my words from time to time, so be it. And if my whoring causes the tiniest bit of discomfort to my husband, then I have done what I can do to help maintain balance." She turned away and walked slowly towards a pink Oleander bush. "What can I possibly do to help you?"

Catherine followed. "Talk to them. Convince them that the marriage is not practical, that my marriage to a lowly prince from England will yield them nothing. The Tudors are not the allies we seek."

Joanna reached out and touched the tender oleander blossoms with the tips of her right fingers. She smiled. "You cannot say these things to them yourself?"

"Yes, I can, and I will if necessary. I will refuse to marry him if it comes to that. But it will mean more coming from you, heir to the throne. My objection will seem like more of the same to them: their youngest and most disruptive child once again bringing shame to the family. But if you speak on my behalf and explain to them that a marriage to the Tudors will be useless, they will listen."

Joanna shook her head. "I'm not certain I agree that the marriage will be useless. The Tudor house is one on the rise. There may be much to gain with a marriage to Arthur."

Catherine's heart sank. She was so mad that she wanted to scream, to cry. Instead, she put her hand on Joanna's back, rubbed her soft shoulder, and said, "Please, Joanna, I beg you. I do not want to marry him. He is a sickly boy - nay, a sick boy - though he denies it." She looked around the courtyard to make sure the guards were out of ear shot. "And his family is aligned with the Eldar Gods. I know it. If he were to die in marriage, then I'd be passed off to Henry, and I'll kill myself before I submit to that brute."

Joanna plucked a stem of bright pink oleander blossoms from the bush. She did not place them on her face, but she held them near her nose and sniffed. She closed her eyes and smiled. "I cannot stand the thought of you dead, sweet sister. You and I, we are truly the last best hope for the House of Aragon. Aren't these beautiful," she asked, presenting the blossoms to Catherine. Catherine reached for them, but Joanna pulled them away. "Beautiful, but deadly."

Joanna let the blossoms drop from her hand. She nodded, turned, and walked away. "Very well, sweet sister, I will speak on your behalf." She giggled. "I will roar like a dragon, and they will hear me. Do not fear, Catherine. I will take care of everything."

An hour later, Arthur Tudor, Prince of Wales, was found dead in his quarters.

*****

They found him hung by the neck from the thick rafters of his room. He was hung so high, they could not figure out how he had gotten up there, for he was not a very tall man. But he swung in the light breeze that flowed through his tiny window, his neck bloody from the rope, his face nice and purple, his tongue extended and bloated like a red beet. There was nothing in the room that had been disturbed or disheveled. It was clean and royally presented. It even had a beautiful bouquet of poppies, roses, and oleander blossoms.

Naturally, they blamed the Muslim, for he had been "seen" near Arthur's quarters just recently. And thus, Fymurip was taken to the gaol on the west side of the palace, and down a dark, damp set of stairs. He was tossed into a cell, much like the ones he had seen at

Marcilla Castle in Navarre. And there he lay, cold and wet, for several hours. How many, he could not say, for he did not remember what time it was when they had taken him, and there was no light save for a slow burning candle on a stool in the far corner.

In time, three guards came and took him out. By then, the sun was setting and sconces along the wall all held burning torches. It was like a fire colonnade, as if he were being taken, hands tied behind his back, to his execution. And perhaps he was, Fymurip thought. He struggled against the guards' hold on him. It was difficult with his hands tied, but he managed once to get away, and they chased him for a few minutes, before he was surrounded, Captain de Onis rounded a corner and struck Fymurip in the head with the hilt of his sword. Dazed and in pain, Fymurip was picked up and dragged to his execution.

But it wasn't his execution. He could see that, as they dragged him through the line of torches, that he was not being taken outside, into the courtyard, or wherever the hooded man might be waiting. Instead, he was taken to King Ferdinand's throne room, and there, waiting for him, was Catherine... and Alfredo.

All three were tied, though the little Trasgo's body was completely wrapped in cord. He lay on the floor at the feet of the king, his mouth filled with a cloth and tied shut. He struggled, though it seemed more from fear than any reasonable attempt at getting free. Fymurip was dragged into the room and laid at Catherine's side.

"I'm sorry," she whispered to him as he tried rising up on his elbows. "I didn't realize what would happen. I'm—"

"Silence!" A guard who stood beside the king and queen bellowed. "You will be silent in the present of your king and queen, until you are given permission to talk."

"This is utter nonsense, Father," Catherine said, ignoring the order. "Fymurip is innocent. He would never do such a thing."

"We will determine his guilt or innocence on our own, my daughter," King Ferdinand said, waving her off. Beside him, Queen Isabella held her tongue, though her expression was one of concern, fear. "Now, my good constable, please read the charge."

The man who had ordered Catherine's silence spoke again. "Fymurip Azat, you have been charged with murdering Arthur, Prince of Wales, who was found in his room, hung by the neck. How do you plead?"

His head and vision were still fuzzy, but Fymurip Azat rose on weak knees. He lifted his bound, shaking hands and pushed away stands of dark hair covering his swollen forehead. He smiled through the pain, and shouted, "Guilty as charged!"

VIII

VIII

A collective gasp filled the room. It was clear to Catherine that no one expected the Saracen to admit his guilt. It was preposterous, in fact.

"What are you doing?" She asked him. "You are not guilty... are you?"

She hated herself for asking the question. Why was she asking the question? She didn't believe that he killed Arthur. The question just came out, and he stared at her, drilling holes in her face with his angry stare. Then he softened, blinked twice, then turned to face the king. "Of course I'm guilty."

"So, you freely admit that you killed the Prince of Wales," the constable said, "and put our country of Spain at great risk of retribution?"

Fymurip shook his head. "No, but if my acceptance of guilt will put an end to this charade, then I will gladly face my end. I am guilty only of being Muslim in Spain, and so of course I'm guilty of Prince Arthur's death. There can be no other explanation given that will sate the wrath and retribution of England. I have to be guilty, don't I? It's the only way to ensure that England doesn't bring death and desolation to your shores.

"So here I am... guilty. Kill me and be done it with. And then let your daughter be free. She is guilty of nothing but being the daughter of a king who—"

"Be still!" Catherine barked at Fymurip. "Do not make it any worse than it already is. You are not guilty; stop being foolish about it." She pulled away from a guard holding her arm and made steps closer to her father. "Fymurip is not guilty of the crime, Father. Can you not see the folly of that declaration? This isn't the work of one lowly Muslim soldier with constant eyes upon him, even while he sleeps. This is Eldar magic."

A few coughing laughs rose among those in attendance. Even the king raised an eyebrow and let a smile creep across his face. Mother sat quietly beside him, neither speaking nor showing any emotion at all. "Eldar magic?" The King chuckled. "There is no Eldar sorcery here, Catherine. This is a Christian realm. There is no super-natural magic of any kind in my castle."

"Then what is that lying at your feet?" She asked. "That is no emissary from Pope Alexander. He is a Trasgo. A goblin. They are not conceived of holy writ, my king. He is a being of pure sorcery."

King Ferdinand ignored the question, clapped his hands to-gether, and from the door through which Queen Isabella had exited previously, came two guards, carrying a long box between them.

They placed the box beside Alfredo and flipped open the top. Inside, on a soft bed of velvet, lay Tizona.

Catherine's heart leapt. She almost felt relief. She approached carefully, wary of the screaming that it would do in her presence. But only a soft, almost tolerable, muffled call for "Colada" came from within the box. "You have figured out a way to keep it from screaming."

Again, the King ignored his daughter's words. "You recognize it. That both pleases and saddens me. This is my sword, Catherine, and it is my right to decide whom to give it to. And yet this goblin tells us that he was there in Marcilla Castle on the night that you took it. I gave it to Pedro de Peralta y Ezpeleta as a gesture of goodwill so that Aragon and Navarre may always be at peace. That goodwill has now been shattered with the theft, by you, of this sword. So how do you plead?"

A guard reached down to Alfredo's face and pulled the gag away from the creature's mouth. Alfredo gulped air and screamed, "I am sorry, dear Catherine. I am so sorry. I came here to free you, to protect you. And they grabbed me. They tortured me. They made me confess."

A guard kicked Alfredo in the gut, and the Trasgo yelped and shuttered at the blow.

Catherine took three steps and then leapt into the air and drove both of her feet into the chest of the offending guard. The man had no time to react, to shield himself from the strike. He fell back hard. He tried keeping his feet, but his boot heel struck the dais on which the king's throne sat, and he fell back into Ferdinand's legs.

The constable rushed the throne to protect the king. The guards rushed Catherine and Fymurip (who was now moving to protect Catherine). They were both tackled to the floor and held there under dozens of bodies. Alfredo was picked up and placed in the pile.

"Let them up!" King Ferdinand said, collecting himself and re-taking the throne. He was disheveled, shocked perhaps, at the speed of his daughter's attack. Perhaps he had no idea just how strong, how skilled, she was. Perhaps he was even afraid of her now, just a little. Good, Catherine thought, as the guards pulled her up and placed her on her knees before her father. I hope he is. He should be.

"You come to my throne -"

"I did not come here. You forced me -"

"- and attack my guard." The king waved off further help. "And you conspire with Muslims and beasts to steal my property —"

"You gave it away, Father. Tizona is no longer yours -"

"Nor is it yours to steal back! How dare you?"

"Listen to me, Father," Catherine said, trying to calm the rage in her voice, "listen. The Eldar Gods want Tizona. That is why the League sent me to Spain, so that I would find it and take it back to them. Let me go. Let us go. Give me the sword and let us complete our mission. For I swear to you, if you allow it to remain in Spain, to remain here, the Eldar Gods will find it, and your reign will fall. You and Mother will die, and everything that you have built, everything that you cherish, everything that you hold holy, will fall to ash."

The king was silent for a long while, and the room seemed to hang on a cliff. Then, he said, with a tiny chuckle, "I should have stopped whelping children before you were born."

Catherine felt tears well in her eyes. She was surprised by it. She thought that nothing this man could say, or do, anymore could make her cry, and she almost let a tear drop. Then she pushed away the pain, and instead, said, "I wish it as well, Father, for what a dis-appointment I have been to you. Here is the sum of it, my Lord. I have laid with heretics. Yes, I have spread my legs for Jews and Mus-lims." She turned to Fymurip. "I have taken this man's seed into my body, and I will do it again, and again and again."

"Catherine, that is enough!" Queen Isabella said, tears now flowing down her face. "Stop lying."

"It is all true, Mother, every word. And it was my fault. I or-dered Fymurip to kill Prince Arthur, for he was ugly and because you wanted me to marry him. But I was not going to live a life like you have: nothing more than a slave to some man's needs. I do what I want, and fuck whom I desire. I ordered Fymurip to kill Prince Ar-thur because I want Spain to fall. And I condemn you, Father. And I condemn your Christian god!"

"Heretic!" King Ferdinand shouted. "You blaspheme before your own father, your mother? I condemn you, you miserable little wretch! Cast these murderers, these thieves, into gaol. And bring me Diego de Deza and my Inquisition. They will burn at the stake for what they have done!"

She and Fymurip were seized and dragged from the throne room. Catherine screamed the entire way, but she never let her eyes off her father, who ignored his wife's pleas for leniency. Catherine spit so that her father could see it: one more disrespect before it all came to an end. And so it would, she knew, for Father never summoned the Inquisition unless he meant to use them. So be it. Catherine would happily die, for if the king of Spain was too stupid, too stubborn, too inflexible to see that soon, his entire reign would fall, then she didn't want to be alive to see her precious country burn.

*****

Fymurip could hear Catherine sobbing. He had listened to it all night, in fact, through the dark damp air of the gaol cell in which they lay. They were not in the same cell. She was across from him, and in the dark, he could not see her, for there were no torches or lanterns. Just darkness and sorrow. For Fymurip felt so much sorrow. Not for the fact that he was in gaol, awaiting the Spanish Inquisition. No. Sorrow for Catherine, for surely the pain she felt was insurmountable and far greater than his.

Her father had disowned her, had told her, in his throne room, in front of his court, that he wished his youngest daughter had never been born. What a terrible, terrible thing to say to a child. Then again, Catherine had not been shy with her words either. She had condemned her father as well, but only in response to his declaration, and was it justified? Fymurip did not know. He had never had to deal with such a dysfunctional family life, one of royalty, ceremony, expectation, and stress.

Fymurip had been born low, and there he had remained. His childhood was not perfect, he remembered. His father had been killed early in Fymurip's life at the so-called Great Stand on the Ugra River against Muscovites. His mother never took up with another man, and thus, he and his siblings had been poor. That's what they were, and that's who they were. There was never any expectation that he or anyone else in the family would make something of themselves, such that life would be a horror, a burden to live. The poor had their troubles, indeed, but it was confined to finding food, work, shelter, and perhaps finding someone to marry. In many ways, Fymurip was glad he had been poor. Allah knew, he had no desire to go through what Catherine was going through right now.

But he wanted to comfort her, to hug her close and tell her that it would be all right. She had put herself in harm's way for him, had confessed (untruthfully) that she had ordered the murder of Prince Arthur. But that was a lie. He hadn't killed Arthur any more than she had. No. If there was anyone to blame, it had to be *Juana la Loca*. It had to be.

But how?

"I am sorry." Catherine's words were soft. "So sorry. This is my fault."

Fymurip shook his head, though she could not see it in the darkness. "No, my lady. It is mine. I was the one who got angry and confessed to a crime I did not commit. I should have kept calm and proclaimed my innocence. Then, you would not have had to confess to things you have never done, just to protect me. But I got angry. I'm tired of people seeing my dark hair, my dark skin, and assuming I am to blame for whatever nefarious things that have happened."

"I should never have brought you to Spain. This was my responsibility, not yours. I had no right to put you in harm's way. I knew how it would be; bringing a Muslim to Spain. But—I wanted you here, beside me, to -"

"I made my choice, Catherine. We make our choices in life, and we must live by those choices. What is done is done. Let us not linger on the past. We must plan for our escape. Do you have a plan?"

"Do you miss your home, Fymurip?" Catherine asked, ignoring his question.

"Yes," Fymurip said. "I do. I haven't seen it in a long time. But I miss the steppe, the flat country. It's bitter cold in the winter, but so pleasant in spring."

"I love Spain," she said, and Fymurip hoped she was smiling. "I do. I love every inch of it. I thought coming back would be the right thing to do, though I knew it was a risk. A risk worth taking. Getting that sword out of here, out of Spain, though it is as much a part of Spain as I am."

"Then let us not dawdle here in the dark. We must escape and—"

"There is no escape, don't you understand? It's over. Diego de Deza will come, and he will bring the Inquisition with him. He will declare us heretics, and we will burn at the stake."

She began to sob again, and Fymurip felt a sinking in his chest. For the first time, real despair set in. Perhaps she was right. Perhaps it was over.

He laid his head down on the cold stone, closed his eyes, and tried to remember his childhood home.

The lock in the door outside his cell in the hallway clapped, and the door creaked open. Fymurip crawled to the bars on hands and knees and peered out. A hooded figure slipped through the door holding a lantern. The person closed the door behind him and raised the lantern up. It was a small person, a little round in the middle, but small. The light spread across the gaol, and Fymurip could see Catherine for the first time in hours. Her face was a smear of tears, her eyes red and swollen.

"Who are you?" Catherine asked through her iron bars, clutching them as if they gave her strength.

The figure removed the hood.

"Mother!"

Queen Isabella stood there, her face not much cleaner than her daughter's. She laid the lantern aside, rummaged around in the pocket of the thick robes that she wore, and pulled out a key. She opened Catherine's cell first, then Fymurip's.

"Mother, I—"

"Shhh!" The queen said, pressing her finger to her lips. "There is no time to talk. Your father is still enraged by your poor behavior. You must go quickly, before he realizes you are gone."

"Why are you doing this?" Catherine asked. "Why are you risking yourself?"

"Because you are my daughter, and I know that you were lying. You did not kill Arthur, nor did you order it. Nor have you laid with all those men." She pressed her hand against Catherine's stomach. "Your belly tells the truth."

"When Father finds out you helped us escape, he'll—"

"I will blame it on the Trasgo, and it will be dead before the sun rises. What troubles you, my daughter? I find it hard to believe that you care so much for a sniveling little beast like it, given your profession."

"I don't, but - but it has helped us, and despite all I know, I now feel responsible for its welfare."

"Grow up, Catherine." Queen Isabella's words were harsh, but nowhere near as harsh as the king's. "You have chosen to live a life to serve a greater purpose. To try to keep the world free of Eldar trappings. And you cannot believe that there will never be casualties along the way. Much must be sacrificed in this war against the Eldar gods, my daughter, and so you cannot cry for the loss of the likes of Alfredo. Yes, I believe in the Eldar Gods. I have seen their devilment up close. And you are right: Spain will fall if El Cid's swords are not taken away and protected."

Queen Isabella removed her robe. On her back, wrapped in velvet, lay Tizona. She too was almost dwarfed by its size, its broad blade that lay across her back. But she handled it well, swung it down off her shoulder, and handed it to Fymurip.

He was reluctant to accept, but the Queen insisted. "Take it. The velvet will protect you from its call as you go to Madrid and take Colada."

And so it was true. As quiet as it was in the throne room, so too was it here. Fymurip took it, and this time, he was able to hold it without falling into deep nausea.

"Colada," Catherine asked. "We are not going for Colada. We are leaving Spain with Tizona alone."

"You must take Colada as well. It is not enough to simply keep one from the other. They must be acquired together and removed from Spain forever, or the Eldar gods will find Colada themselves, and God only knows what they will do with it. You are the only one who can do this; the only one I trust. You have the power and strength to see it through. Remember, my daughter. Remember what Georg's note said: *El dragon no puede levantarse*."

Catherine flung herself into her mother's arms and hugged her tightly. "Thank you, Mama. I'm so sorry for what I said. I— where are our swords? We need our swords."

"There are two fresh horses being held for you at the gate. Your swords are already on them." She pushed Catherine away. "Go, now, before it is too late."

Before they left the gaol, Queen Isabella grabbed Fymurip's arm, squeezed it harder than he would have imagined, and said, "Protect her, Fymurip Azat. I order you to keep my daughter safe."

Fymurip nodded. "Yes, my Lady. With all my strength."

They left, quietly, keeping low and to the walls as they moved up staircases, through dark hallways, and towards the front gate.

IX

From the ramparts of El Palacio de la Aljafería, Queen Isabella watched her daughter and Fymurip Azat flee for their lives across the bridge. She watched until they were no longer visible in the rising light of dawn. "I have sent my daughter to her death," she said quietly to the small Trasgo named Alfredo at her side. She tried not to show her tears. "I have sent her to her death."

"On the contrary, my queen," Alfredo said. "You have done a great service to the Eldar gods."

"The devil, you mean." For was there a difference between him and the Eldar gods? Not in Queen Isabella's mind, at least. One devil was much the same as the next. And try as she might her whole life to fight against him, to construct entire kingdoms devoted to destroying him, she had realized once and for all, many years ago, that she was not strong enough to fight them both. Despite her outward appearance of unwavering devotion to God, she had to make a choice. She made it, and now, their payment was due. "I do not see how putting those hateful swords together will do good service to anyone."

"Then let me educate you, my queen," Alfredo said. "If you and King Ferdinand wish to maintain your hold on the throne of Spain and solidify your growing power in the New World, then the Turks must fall. There is no army strong enough to face it on earth, and as long as they control the Middle East and Eastern Europe, the Eldar gods will never be at peace, and neither will you. They have given you your power. Now it is time to give back."

"Catherine isn't strong enough. She will die before she completes the mission."

Alfredo shook his head. "I have never seen a woman that young and that capable. And I have never seen Tizona cry for Colada so loudly as it does in her presence and in the presence of that Tatar. They were born to wield those swords. It's the only way."

El dragon no puede levantarse, Queen Isabella said.

"No, my good queen. *El dragon hay que levantarse*. The dragon must rise! If you wish to keep your throne, to preserve your family's power, than the Mamluks must defeat the Turks in the Levant. And soon. The Eldar gods grow impatient. If they cannot win there, then I guarantee you that they will win here. The choice is yours, my Lady. Make it."

Sniveling little cretin. Isabella had a good mind to call for the guards and have this thing beaten to death, just as she had promised Catherine. But that would only bring her more misery. And this Trasgo was the least of her worries now.

Joanna knows! Her first daughter, in line to rule, had killed Prince Arthur. But how? And how had she strung the body up so high? Were there competing interests among the Eldar gods? And was Joanna on their side, against her mother, her father, just as Catherine was now? Isabella shook her head, fear rising with her heartbeats. Everything seemed to be falling apart.

"Very well," she said. "I will try to call off Diego de Deza and his dogs, but it may be too late. If so, you promise me that Catherine will live regardless?"

Alfredo bowed and made a motion as if he were sweeping the air with a hat. "I give you my word, my Lady. It is in my nature to serve and protect. And so you must bid me farewell. I'm off to serve our mutual interests."

Alfredo dropped down from his perch and made away quickly.

Queen Isabella looked back towards the road down which Catherine had fled. She blew her daughter a kiss, wiped away a tear, and turned away.

Soon, King Ferdinand would be awake, and she'd have another devil to treat with.

*****

Three miles from the palace, Fymurip pulled the rein on his horse and stopped.

Catherine trotted another fifty yards before she realized it. Then she stopped, turned her horse, and went to him. "Why have you stopped? We must keep going."

"Let's talk, Catherine," he said.

"No," she replied, "we can discuss whatever it is you wish, but further down the road. My father will realize we're gone soon and—"

"No! We speak now."

He dropped from his saddle, thankful that his sword and dagger were tucked securely beneath it. He never felt good without them.

"Very well," Catherine said, dismounting. "What do you want?"

"*El dragon no puede levantarse*," Fymurip said. "Your sister said it in the courtyard, and you said it was nothing. Your mother said it right before we left. What does it mean, Catherine? I will not get back on my horse until you tell me."

He stared at her, and he could see that the question made her uncomfortable. She was afraid.

She sighed deeply, nodded, bent down, and pulled a small piece of paper from her boot. He remembered it: Georg Cromer's letter that she had received in Avignon from the Hanseatic League informant.

She handed it to him. It was weathered, dirty, and worn with sweat. He opened it and read the same words he had just uttered.

"There is a myth about El Cid, Fymurip," Catherine said, "one that until recently, I never believed. It is true that the record claims that *Rodrigo Díaz de Vivar* was one of the greatest warriors in all of Spain, and that he fought for both sides on many occasions. That is in the historical record and agreed upon by scholars everywhere. But what the public record never says is that at the Battle of Alcaraz, their Muslim counterpart, Al-Mustain, employed a Cuélebre, a dragon, to help defeat El Cid and his ally Pedro I of Aragon. I have no idea where he acquired such a beast. The truth of that has been lost to the ages.

"The Christians were being slaughtered by this dragon, and only El Cid seemed strong enough to face it. They fought, for days, across the bloody field, until finally El Cid, wielding both Tizona and Colada, struck a mighty blow against the dragon and tore its head from its body. El Cid then proceeded to hack the dragon's body to tiny pieces, so as not to leave any part capable of rising again to fight.

"And so, the battle was won. But there ever after, did El Cid change. He was not himself; he was distant, preoccupied, out of focus. And not long afterwards, he fought his last battle, and shortly thereafter, he died. But always did the swords, even after his death, call to one another, no matter how far apart they were. Sometimes their voices were strong; sometimes, weaker, but constant.

"Something happened to those swords, Fymurip, in killing that dragon. And now, the Eldar gods want them. For what purpose I honestly do not know. But they are seeking them both. I'm certain of that now. We have to find Colada and take it away as well."

The revelation struck Fymurip like a rock. He felt like sitting down. He wiped cold sweat from his head. "And you did not feel the need to tell me about this when you got the message from Georg? This did not occur to you at all?"

Catherine nodded. "Of course, it did. But I don't know why I didn't tell you. I didn't believe it at first. I figured Georg was just being superstitious, foolish to believe such nonsense. But when I finally heard Tizona's call, I guess I began to doubt my own beliefs. But still, I didn't want to remain in Spain any longer than we had to; I did not want to face my father. Our mission was to find Tizona, and we did. But now, I'm not so sure. Just one of El Cid's swords in the hands of Eldar priests… the thought of it is terrifying. Whatever it is they plan to do with these swords, we have to stop it. The only way to do that is to take them both as far away as we can."

She stopped and Fymurip felt like climbing on his horse, turning north, and returning to France. The swords be damned. At first, he had been the one advocating going after Colada. Now Catherine was, and he had no desire to do it. A dragon! Gods be good, but the stories behind those horrid beasts stretched from one end of the world to the other. In ancient times, entire cities burned to the ground from their fire. People in villages were swallowed whole by just one such beast. And Fymurip had always been glad that those stories were just…stories. Maybe they were not stories at all.

What to do? Fymurip could see the answer in Catherine's weary, bloodshot eyes: she was going after Colada, with or without him. Queen Isabella's order to him to protect her daughter rang clearly in his mind, and he wanted to follow it. But a dragon?

He went to his saddle. There lay Tizona wrapped tightly in velvet. He put his ear to it. Its voice was faint, but there, always there as Catherine had said. And it would always be there if it was never reunited with Colada. No matter where it was, it would always wail. Fymurip climbed on his horse. He grabbed the reins and said, "Very well, Catherine. Let's go to Madrid and find that cursed sword. But never keep anything from me again. If we are to be partners, I must know everything. Agreed?"

Catherine nodded. "I promise."

They guided their horses back into the road. Fymurip let Catherine take the lead, for this was her home, her country, and if she was insistent on going to Madrid, he would let her lead the way.

Part Three

Colada Calling

I

Cherubs bit at Katherine's heels as she whipped her horse down a narrow path and through a thick forest. There were a dozen at least, though it was impossible to discern their actual count due to the brilliant white light emanating from within their chests. Their plump little boy bodies sagged beneath their wings, which worked diligently to keep them aloft and at Catherine's sides. Her horse was faring no better, as the Cherubs' sharp, deadly teeth nipped at its hide, its neck and haunches, keeping it off balance and slow.

"What are these things?" Fymurip asked. He fought for his life too, about twenty paces behind her. There were at least another dozen or more nipping at his horse. The Tatar had decided to drop his reins, keep a tight hold on his horse with his strong thigh muscles, and then use both sword and dagger to knock the little beasts senseless. He was fairing only slightly better than Catherine.

"Cherubs," she shouted as she grabbed one of them in her left hand and squeezed. Its head bulged like a bladder; its eyes bugged. It tried wiggling free, tried biting the soft tissue between thumb and forefinger. She turned her hand, squeezed tighter, and slammed it into her saddle. It did not bleed, but the force of the blow made it pop like a grape. A blinding white flash came from within, and then it was gone, only to be replaced by another. She wiped her hand clean of its white, radiant fluid on her pant leg, and then fought off others like swiping flies. "Cherubs... from the Inquisition."

So, her father had followed through with what he had ordered: he'd sent the Inquisition after them.

As she fought them off as best she could, she kept looking behind them, to the sides along the wooded path, to see if anyone was chasing them, or hiding in ambush. No one so far, but she knew that would not last. The purpose of the Cherubs was not to kill them, but to delay, and if it was God's will, force them to go forward on foot. Their real targets were the horses, but in the chaos of battle, the little things didn't distinguish between a bite of horse and a bite of human flesh. They weren't smart enough to make the distinction. They were tools of the Inquisition and agents of God, or, at least, the God that Christians worshipped. They were thralls more than anything, having little say in what they could and could not do. Someone had ordered them to find and attack her and Fymurip. That meant the Inquisition was near, and once they were on your tail, they were rarely shaken away.

But right now, she needed to change the nature of this chase. It seemed that the harder they tried to run, more and more piled on, forming out of the swirling dust of the path. And they were bright, so bright as to make it near impossible to see. Something had to change. "Follow me!" She shouted over the Cherub's annoying screeching voices, which blended together to form an almost demonic chorus.

Catherine pulled her reins to the right and forced her horse into the wood and through the underbrush. Her horse struck the brush and, like a hand working down a branch to remove even smaller branches, the Cherubs were left behind in a screaming, mangled pile. Fymurip did the same, but his horse hit a larger, thicker patch of brush, and baulked. Some of the Cherubs in pursuit fell away, but others stayed. The horse whinnied, fought against moving any further, and Fymurip was tossed from the saddle.

He struck the ground hard, but luckily it was soft and covered with decaying leaves and roots. He shouted when he struck, but rolled, stopped his descent into a gully, and came up with his blades ready.

Catherine dismounted, grabbed her own sword, and worked her way towards Fymurip as the rest of the Cherubs still on Fymurip's horse began to feast in sprays of blood and torn muscle. It was sickening and gave new meaning to the blood of Christ. Catherine tried to ignore it all.

They stood back to back, blades ready, waiting. "Will they come at us again?"

"I don't know," Catherine said. "They got what they wanted, the horses."

"Tizona!" Fymurip said, pointing at his horse that was slowly being consumed by the Cherubs. "We must not let them take it."

"They won't," Catherine said. "It is too big, too heavy for them to carry. Besides, look at them, they are avoiding the saddle."

The Cherubs worked over the horse, save for the middle where the girth strap of the saddle was still in place. Underneath it, wedged against the horse's chest, lay El Cid's sword, still wrapped in velvet.

"I have an idea." Fymurip said. He dropped his blades and walked towards the horse.

"What are you doing?"

Fymurip ignored her and kept walking. When he drew close to the carcass of the horse, some of the Cherubs changed their attention to him and began nipping at his arms. He fought them off as best he could, but endured their bites until he reached the saddle, pulled the girth strap up, and drew Tizona.

The velvet was kept in place by strong goat hide, wrapped tightly from tip to hilt. Fymurip did not bother trying to remove it, to free the blade of its bindings. Made sense to Catherine, for it was the only way he could hold it without falling into nausea. He took the blade firmly in both hands, held it high, and then began to swing it through the bodies of the Cherubs.

Each winged creature struck by the blade exploded in a sharp, blinding flash, one after the other, like eggs breaking against a wall. Two swings later and the Cherubs finally realized what was happening, and those still alive flew up from their feast and disappeared in the growing storm clouds. Three more swings and all were gone. Fymurip took a couple more swings through empty air and then realized that it was over. He fell to a knee. Catherine was at his side.

"They're gone," she said, guiding him to sit on the ground near his destroyed horse. "They are not likely to come back."

"Why?"

"Because of that," she said, pointing at Tizona which lay in his lap. "They cannot fight against it, clearly, and now they know. But they were going after our horses. They have succeeded. But with that sword, with what it can do, the Inquisition will not send them back. They'll bring themselves next time."

"I feel a little light-headed," Fymurip said. "I guess Tizona is still making me ill even with the velvet."

Catherine shook her head. "No. Cherub bites can be a little intoxicating, almost euphoric. What you are feeling is a growing love for Christ. It is in their blood. A few more bites, and you might have become a Christian."

Fymurip snickered. "Well, let's make sure that never happens."

"You wielded it well. Tizona, I mean."

"I've been working with blades all my life."

"No, it was more. For a moment, I could not tell the difference between your arm and the blade."

Fymurip nodded. "It did feel right, I must say. Good balance, excellent grip on the hilt. Almost made for my hand."

That thought scared her, but she kept her fears to herself. "Come," she said, not wanting to explore the matter any further. "It'll rain soon, and we're not far from Madrid. We might be able to find my horse if it survived. If not, we'll keep under brush. It'll be slower, but better. Less eyes upon us."

She helped him to his feet. It began to rain.

About a quarter mile further through the forest, they found her horse, lying dead in a small brook, with Cherub bites all along its flank. A few Cherubs had lingered to feast on the blood, but once they saw Catherine and Fymurip, they fled without support of larger numbers.

Another mile of travel beneath the canopy of trees and crows began to caw madly. Their echo was almost as terrifying as the Cherubs' shrieking choir of voices. But it was just noise. No flocks of black birds descended upon them as they moved, and Catherine was both relieved and terrified. She kept an eye constantly towards the dark boughs above them.

Christian eyes may not be upon us, she thought, *but who else is watching?*

*****

They arrived within sight of The Royal Alcazar of Madrid, or the Real Alcazar de Madrid, by dusk, stretched, worn, and exhausted. But they were alive, and Fymurip found comfort in that. The effects of the Cherub bites had worn off, and he had regained much of his strength, though like Catherine, he wavered on weak legs. Both of them were spent, and there would be no attempt at finding Colada tonight.

"Where do we go now?" Fymurip asked as they paused about a mile from the Alcazar. Torch and lantern light gave the structure shape in the darkness for them to see it clearly; clear enough at least to know that tomorrow's attempt at breaking in would be difficult at best. In many ways, it reminded Fymurip of Marcilla Castle. Like that one, it too was square, but its walls were taller, its battlements thicker. It was indeed a mighty fortress.

"I know a man," Catherine said, "a monk. He'll help us."

"I hope he doesn't offer the same kind of help that the Inquisition did on the road," Fymurip said, trying to lighten the mood. He was still a little punchy from the Cherub intoxication.

"Don't be silly. Come."

They kept to the tree line as they moved closer to Madrid itself. There were many people out and about, more so than they had seen in Marcilla. The roads in and out of Madrid were filled with carts and folks moving by horse and by foot. Madrid was growing fast; Catherine had told him as they made their way through the forest. And that was both good and bad, she said.

The original Alcazar had been built by Amir Muhammad I of Cordoba almost 700 years ago, to serve as the central location of the Islamic citadel of Mayrit, which also included in those days a walled courtyard, a mosque, and the home of the Amir himself. But after the Reconquista, her father and mother had claimed it for their own, and lived and worked there most often, despite its rather small facade, and the constant construction that they had ordered to bring it up to their standards, and presumably, the standards of any future kings and queens of Spain. Her parents liked the location more so than Zaragoza because Madrid was more centrally located, which provided natural protection against invaders, and it also gave them better coordination for ground forces and for their Inquisition. Being able to send out Diego de Deza and his swine, Catherine said, was the bad part of Madrid growing so quickly over the last few years. It meant that the Inquisition held Madrid as its base of operation. It also meant that Madrid had become an important place for the Catholic Church. She and Fymurip would get no support here.

"Then why do we seek out a monk?" Fymurip asked.

"I've known him since I was a child. He is a good man, a Godly man if that means anything in this world anymore. He will help us."

They moved as quickly as they could, around the city, out of sight of anyone that seemed lecherous. There were a lot of those folk wandering about, especially as the sun set. One such man tried to accost Catherine as they turned a corner. He got his manhood shoved back into his crotch by a swift knee. Thereafter, no one bothered them.

They turned another corner, and there it lay, a large monastery that Catherine called the Hieronymus. Fymurip thought about pressing her for more information but thought better of it as they approached its thick double-wide door. To Fymurip's eyes it was simply another Christian artifice filled with people that would not like him on principle, no matter how generous they might seem to his face. But he followed her anyway, until they were at the door, and Catherine grabbed the large knocker and gave it three strong taps.

Two more taps later and a tiny man wearing a brown cowl opened the door. "Good evening. We are here to see Bartolome de Huerva."

"Do you have an appointment, miss?" the man asked.

Even from his place behind Catherine's back, Fymurip could smell food on the man's breath. There was also a hint of alcohol, a mead or a heavy ale. Perhaps he had just finished dining. The thought of food sounded good to Fymurip. They hadn't eaten in a while.

"An appointment is unnecessary," she said. "Tell him... Catherine, daughter of King Ferdinand and Queen Isabella, wishes to speak with him."

The man's eyes grew wide, and he bowed multiple times. "Yes, Lady Catherine. I apologize. It has been a long time since—"

"My good man, haste is necessary," she said, pushing the man politely back a couple paces. "We must see him now."

The man bowed once again, turned, and shuffled away, leaving the door open for them. Fymurip was glad Catherine had sent him away, for one more scent of food and he'd have collapsed at the stoop. His stomach growled. Catherine noticed.

"Do you drink wine? Is it haram?"

Fymurip was impressed. Catherine had taken the time to learn some Islamic Law. Where she had gotten that knowledge, he did not know. Perhaps she had been aware for a long time; she had travelled almost all of Europe in some capacity or another, and she was Spanish and not too far from Moorish occupation. Surely, he had not been the only Muslim person that she had encountered, although she had never said anything about meeting others.

"Yes, alcohol is forbidden. But I have been known to violate the precepts of my faith on occasion, and if the only thing these monks have to drink is wine, then I shall drown in it. I may also dirty my body with pig meat if that's the only food—"

"Do not fear, my friend," Catherine said, smiling and chuckling despite her utter exhaustion, "I will not allow these men to violate who you are any more than you are willing. I'm sure they have less egregious food selections for your ravenous state."

The light of the foyer in which they waited was low, and so Fymurip could not see the wonderful architecture of the monastery, nor the murals of God and his angels painted across the walls and arched ceiling. Despite her assurances, Fymurip felt uncomfortable. He had travelled far with Lux von Junker, and he was a Christian warrior. But Lux was a lot like Fymurip in that he set aside his faith when the circumstances called for it, and he never behaved in an overly pious manner. Nor did Catherine, for that matter, but this was only the second time Fymurip had stepped into a structure dedicated solely to the Christian god. A wave of unease spread through his body like warm wine. He suddenly realized that he was standing at the center of the struggle between Christianity and Islam in Europe. It did not feel pleasant.

But he bore it well and waited alongside Catherine until an old man appeared. Old to Fymurip anyway, though he was much younger than the man who had greeted them at the door. He was not stooped like the former, and his clothing was a mixture of brown and white, full length with a hood pushed back to reveal hair shaved to mimic a halo. He was darker-skinned than Fymurip would have expected, and he wondered if Bartolome de Huerva had some Moorish blood. That was possible, for the occupation of Spain had lasted so long. But everything else about him was Christian and pious. He was tall and thin with an air of calm dignity. Fymurip could not help but feel comfortable in the man's presence.

Bartolome de Huerva bowed before Catherine. She approached him slowly. He opened his arms. They embraced and kissed each other on the cheeks. De Huerva spoke first.

"It is a joy to see you again, Catherine. We Hieronymites have worried and prayed for your safety."

Catherine nodded. "Thank you, Bartolome. I have missed you as well." She turned to Fymurip. "This is my friend and companion, Fymurip Azat. We are here on important business. We need your help."

Her abruptness seemed to surprise de Huerva, as he stepped closer to Fymurip and cautiously looked at him as if he were a dangerous prize. He squinted. "Well, it seems, my Lady. Cherub bites?"

"Yes," Catherine answered for Fymurip. "I have them too."

De Huerva's ears perked up. "What is that I hear? A faint voice in the air."

Fymurip turned to show his back. "Tizona."

The monk stepped back and glared at Catherine. "You bring that cursed blade here, to my monastery?"

"I thought this was God's house, Bartolome," Catherine said.

"Please, child, do not patronize me. You know exactly what I mean. You come to me with marks from the Inquisition. You bring to me a Saracen carrying El Cid's sword that mewls like a devil baby. I am no fool, Catherine, and word travels fast. Your father seeks that sword, as he seeks you and your companion. I don't know what I can do for you that would not put me and mine at great risk. This is God's house, indeed, but I am in charge of it."

Fymurip could see Catherine's cheek muscles moving. Her eyelids blinked rapidly; a clear sign that she was trying to contain her anger. "You owe me a favor, Bartolome. You owe my family."

The monk huffed. "Your family? It's scattered to the wind. Your sister mumbles mad phrases while plucking flowers. Your mother and father would see you captured and - God forbid - burned at the stake. And you travel with heretics and demon swords and ask for my help. Which part of your family do I owe the most loyalty?"

Catherine stepped closer to the monk, her dark eyes peering up into his. Her face was still, her expression granite. She placed a hand on the hilt of her sword. "The one that stands before you now. Where is that kind, gentle monk that I knew in my youth?"

De Huerva shook his head. "The world has changed, young lady, since you left."

"Indeed, it has, my friend. But I have promised this – Saracen - as you call him, that we can find comfort and protection here, because the man I once knew would never leave a needy soul at the doorstep. Yes, the world has changed, Bartolome, and more than ever, it needs strong, honorable men like you to ensure that it does not slip into utter darkness. If you truly wish to serve God, to serve Spain, then help us now."

De Huerva fell silent, and Fymurip breathed deeply, on a knife edge, waiting for where the shoe might drop. Finally, the monk sighed, shook his head, and said, "Very well. What is it you want, Catherine?"

"Food, a place to rest for the evening, and then tomorrow, entry into the Alcazar. There is a new monastery being constructed within its walls, yes? Then you can gain access readily without drawing the suspicion of the guards. I will accompany you. We will be in and out quickly."

De Huerva nodded. "And why do you need entry to the fortress?"

Catherine looked at Fymurip, then de Huerva. "We have Tizona... we need Colada as well."

The monk turned pale. "You're mad."

Catherine nodded. "Yes, and I'll be mumbling mad things to my own flowers soon enough. But that is our need. Will you help or no?"

De Huerva paused again. He turned, walked a few paces while mumbling to himself. Fymurip tried to hear what the old man was saying. Not Spanish. Perhaps Greek, but more likely Latin or some mixture thereof. Fymurip had heard it spoken before, but he was by no means an expert.

Finally, de Huerva made the cross over his chest, turned, and said, "Yes, I will help, though God may strike me dead. But I cannot give your companion rest. I apologize, Catherine, but he cannot stay." He turned to Fymurip. "You may break bread with us, but then you must go."

"Where?" Catherine asked.

De Huerva blinked. "I know a place."

II

The "place" that de Huerva mentioned was a dilapidated stone hovel on the outskirts of Madrid. Perhaps it had once housed a family of modest means, but now, it lay in ruin, though it was obvious to Fymurip that others had stayed there. De Huerva and his Hieronymite monks must have used it for other travelers as well, those unworthy to reside in the relative comfort behind their monetary walls—a Saracen like Fymurip.

Catherine had first refused to stay at the monastery without her companion, but Fymurip had convinced her to reconsider. It was she who needed the best rest and food, for she would be heading alone into the Royal Alcazar tomorrow with de Huerva. Despite the warning in his heart, Fymurip agreed that it was the best plan. De Huerva could easily pass the guards with Catherine dressed as a monk, her hood pulled down such that her gender and identity unseen. But Fymurip would be another matter entirely.

So here he sat, in the fading light of a lantern, beside an old wooden three-legged table, his belly full, his mind racing, staring at Tizona as it hummed and hummed the name of its lost companion. And for the first time in their travels with the blade, Fymurip felt sorry for it.

It was a foolish feeling, he realized, for Islam teaches that idolatry, or shirk, is the sin of the deification or worship of anything besides Allah. His feeling of sorrow for Tizona was not strictly idolatry, true, but he was placing human feelings upon an artifact when those feelings should be reserved for human endeavors and human souls. A blade was nothing more than forged steel shaped and sharpened to kill, and the sword before him had done its fair share of killing. And what of the story that Catherine had told him about how El Cid had vanquished a dragon with Tizona and Colada together? Now it called to Colada like a mewling babe, as de Huerva had said. How could someone with any feeling at all not pity the poor thing?

But what did the mewling mean? Why did Tizona call for Colada? And presumably, why did Colada do the same in reverse? Why? What had happened when those two swords met to kill the

Cuélebre? There were many questions unanswered, and perhaps light would be shed once the two swords were reunited.

Fymurip reached out and touched the velvet wrapped around Tizona. He touched it carefully with one finger first, then another, and then his entire hand. Its cry for Colada grew louder, but there was no nausea or sickness, thankfully. When he had swung the blade against the Cherubs, he had been holding the hilt, and so he wasn't sure if touching the actual blade would be different. It wasn't. Touching it felt fine. And it had felt fine being swung against the Cherubs, too, more so than he wanted to admit to Catherine. It felt real, natural, as if the blade had been forged for his hand.

"Fymurip!"

He pulled his hand away and stood quickly. He fell back into a stack of dry rotting slats against the shack wall. His mouth open, his heart racing. "What... what did you say?"

He waited for the blade to speak as if it were a person, as if it were Catherine asking a question. But it just lay there, still and innocent, and all he could hear now was "Colada Colada Colada" over and over, as he had for weeks.

Fymurip shook his head. "The wine must have taken me," he said to himself. He had violated haram and had drunk more than he had wanted to, but the bread and cheese tasted better with it, and the goose, and the pig. He shook his head again. I'm tired. I'm hearing things.

Fymurip stared at Tizona for a while longer, but he did not hear his name again.

He collected himself and dared to grab Tizona and place it beside his sword and dagger on the bedroll de Huerva had provide him. He sat down beside them, leaned over, and blew out the lantern, and then lay down to try and sleep.

He slept on and off throughout the cool night. His dreams were fitful.

When he awoke, he was surrounded by several men, in dark clothing, with black scarves covering their faces.

He grabbed for his swords, but they were not there. Strong hands held him down.

"Unhand me! Who are you?" Fymurip struggled against their strength.

A familiar face emerged from those crowded around, a small shadow against the faint light emanating through the hovel window.

The face smiled, showing yellow, crooked teeth.

"Alfredo."

The little Trasgo bowed. "Nice to see you again, Fymurip, sir."

Fymurip tried rising. The hands kept him down. "How did you escape? Why are you here? Why—"

Alfredo waved him silent. "No talking. Now, we wait."

"Wait for what?"

Alfredo smiled. "For Colada."

*****

Catherine had been in the Alcázar Real de Madrid on many occasions. But it had been a long time, and much of it was now under new construction and covered with scaffolding. Artisans, laborers, and common folks scampered about with their various duties, hardly giving any thought to a monk and his hooded companion, as they scampered past guards and made their way across the foundation of the new monastery. As they passed, Catherine marveled at the architecture already constructed on the site. When it was finished, it would be a most beautiful building, and perhaps she would be back someday to see it on full display.

"If any of these guards look at me cross-eyed," Catherine said, "I'll bring them down."

"You would kill honest, Christian men, who are simply doing their duty on behalf of your father?" De Huerva asked.

Catherine nodded, though she doubted the monk saw the gesture through her hood. "Honest? Doubtful. Christian? Perhaps, though I would question their devotion if I were you. One move against me, Bartolome, and I'll strike them down. I'll have no patience today for chicanery."

Her words were both threat and promise. Her sword was tucked underneath her brown habit and ready. She would strike if threatened. But she hoped that her warning would suffice, that Bartolome would take her safely, without complication, to Colada. She hoped that Bartolome's intransigence and hostility last night was simply for Fymurip's benefit, to scare the "Saracen" into some form of submission. Fymurip was not easily scared, she knew. Nor was she, and if necessary, she would put Bartolome under the blade as well. She did not come out and threaten him directly, of course. That would be foolish. But she hoped that beneath her words, he understood their implied meaning.

"Do you know where the sword is, my Lady?"

"Yes. Once inside, I'll lead the way."

They passed the guards at the opening where the monastery's secondary door would lead directly into the Alcazar. It too was still under construction, and so they walked carefully through a maze of workers. Catherine kept her head low, her eyes forward, letting de Huerva lead them into the Alcazar itself.

Once inside, de Huerva paused and stepped aside. Catherine accepted the lead, looked around carefully, saw that there was no one within sight. She pushed her hood back, exposing her face to the cooler air of the castle. She breathed relief, shook her head a little. "So hot. How do you monks stand it?"

"If you love God, my Lady, as we do, the mild discomfort of heat is no burden."

That was a jab at her directly, Catherine knew. But she let it go, ruffled her hair out to give it more air, tucked it back underneath the hood, then pointed to the right. "This way. And please be quiet."

When the king and queen were in Zaragoza, their personal security were with them, and so, today the Alcázar had only a small guard detail inside. The stronger presence outside was simply to keep undesirables - like her - from wandering into the construction areas and disrupting the workers. Now that they were in, there were only a few people scattered here and there: maids, kitchen help, a posted guardsman with a spear and small rapier upon his belt. Nothing that Catherine could not deal with if necessary. But the going was slow because of de Huerva. He kept pausing and speaking to those they passed. Catherine, then, had to pause as well, holding herself still next to the monk as if she were his simple, obedient acolyte. The delay began to annoy.

"You stop once more to chat," she said, as they pressed on, "and I'll run you through."

"I am a servant of God, my Lady, and a servant of the crown. When in the Alcazar, I must greet everyone as equals and hear their burdens if they have any."

Luckily, they were close, or Catherine would have argued further. She rolled her eyes, fixed her hood to ensure her face was shrouded, then turned another corner. At the very end of the long hallway before them stood the door to her parents' personal storage room.

Her mother, especially, had brought a lot of personal items to the marriage, and had also accumulated gifts during her reign as queen. There seemed to be no end to the subjects who wanted to ingratiate themselves to the Spanish crown.

Their way was unhindered as they walked towards the storage room door. Catherine was surprised that there was no one guarding the door, as there were - or, used to be - valuable items within. Perhaps they had moved them to a more secure location. Catherine's heart leapt into her throat. It had been a long time since her last visit, and longer still since she had been in this storage room. Perhaps Colada was no longer there.

"Why are there no guards?" She asked aloud.

De Huerva shook his head. "I do not know, my Lady. I never venture into this part of the castle."

That was a lie, Catherine knew. Perhaps the monk had never been in the royal storage room, but she remembered distinctly de Huerva and other Hieronymite monks walking all the halls of the Alcázar. She stared at him carefully, trying to divine his true intensions. His face was wrinkled, dark, leathery, but honest. At least, it showed no anxiety, no stress.

They reached the door. It was locked with a large piece of iron. She tugged at it and heard the echo of it scraping against the latch. "Locked," she said.

"Then we should depart," de Huerva said, looking down the hallway. "If we break in, they'll hear and—"

"I've not come all this way just to turn and run. Step aside."

De Huerva did so, and Catherine reached under her robe and pulled a knife from her belt. It wasn't the best, sharpest blade she'd ever wielded, but it would suffice. With it gripped firmly, she turned to the door and jammed the blade into the wood behind the latch. The iron lock itself was far too strong to break, but the door, though made of strong, thick oak, was malleable. She worked the blade into the wood, made a good puncture, and then pulled back on the hilt. The iron latch wrenched as the wood behind it splintered. Catherine paused each time she pulled the hilt towards her to let the echo of splintering wood subside. Three more tugs, and the latch broke free from the wood and fell to the floor.

Instinctively, she crouched at the loud sound the iron latch and lock made as they struck the stones at her feet. Luckily, there were no other entranceways into the hallway where they stood. The only way in was from where they had come. If the sound did alert guards, there was no way out but to fight. But no one came, the echo dissipated, and Catherine opened the door.

It was dark, but the light from the hallway filtered into the room enough to let them see inside a few feet. An old and musty smell struck Catherine's face. A scent of mold too, and as she worked her way into the room, she could see moisture along the stone walls. Wooden crates were stacked against the far wall and in the center of the room. A shelf lay against the wall on the left, and there were a few choice pieces of china, glass lamps, and bundled quilts stacked to the ceiling. There were no rodents, Catherine noticed, nor any insects or burrowing creatures of any kind. She was thankful of that. The best pieces of her mother's fortune were gone, however, and what remained were things that she clearly could live without.

"It is empty, my Lady," de Huerva said. "No sword. Let us go."

"Quiet and be still."

Catherine took another three steps into the room, into a place where the light from the hallway had not reached. "Open the door a little farther, will you please?" she asked. "We need more light."

De Huerva sighed so loud that it echoed through the room. Catherine ignored it and waited for the monk to comply. He did and more light filtered in; not a lot, but enough for her to see what she had been looking for.

A full suit of plate armor held up on a metal stand that served as its spine. It almost looked lifelike, and as a child, she remembered being afraid of it, as if some ghost lived inside that would animate the suit and chase after her. But it lay still and quiet, splendid in its strength and size, though the moisture in the air of the room had rusted its sallet, bevor, and cuirass. Its pauldrons held the Castilian Coat-of-Arms, faded and scraped away as if a sword blow had done its worst on the battlefield. Whose suit it belonged to; Catherine did not know. The warrior was long dead. Could it have been El Cid himself? Perhaps, for he had been a Castilian nobleman. It was unlikely, of course, for even with its rust and stiffness from lack of use, it was too new, in too good of shape to have lasted from El Cid's time. Then again, Tizona had endured.

Catherine knelt down and looked at its right gauntlet. In its grip lay a sword.

She reached for it. She touched the hilt and heard the word "Tizona Tizona Tizona," over and over again, growing stronger and louder in her mind with each utterance. A wave of nausea struck her and she fell to the floor.

"Are you all right, my Lady?" de Huerva asked, rushing forward in aide.

Catherine waved him off. "Wait… I'm all right. I'm fine."

The nausea subsided, though the sword's bleated call for Tizona remained. She dared to reach out for it again. Another wave of nausea struck, and then it was gone. She climbed up onto her knees, pulled the stiff, metal fingers of the gauntlet away, and pulled Colada free.

It was a long blade and tarnished from sitting in a dark, wet place. But no rust, thankfully. Its hilt was simple, just a piece of tough black leather wrapped tightly around a smooth metal handle. The hand guard was simple too; just enough to keep the wielder free from counter slashes. The blade, though longer than she was used to, felt good, balanced in her hands, and it appeared as if only one side of its edge had been consistently sharpened, as if its purpose was to attack the enemy from higher ground. Clearly, El Cid had used Colada for hacking at enemy heads while on horseback. Tizona was for stabbing; Colada for slashing.

"Is that it?" de Huerva asked. His voice carried an edge of anxiousness, worry.

Catherine nodded. "Yes."

"Then let us be off."

There was logic in de Huerva's request. To linger meant a greater chance for guardsmen to wander by. But she took a moment to search for the scabbard. She looked in the crates near the armor and behind it. She looked everywhere. Nothing. It seemed odd that such an important and valiant sword did not have a home in which to rest, but she could not search any longer. She'd have to simply tuck it underneath her habit and try not to look funny when walking out.

"Let us go."

De Huerva stepped aside to let Catherine lead the way.

Outside the room, in the hallway, stood twenty men. Catherine halted and looked at their faces. She recognized them immediately.

The workers from outside the new monastery door. And they held swords, spears, and clubs.

"I lied to you, my Lady," de Huerva said as he emerged from the storage. "I asked you last night what member of your family do I serve? You chose yourself, but that is not true. The real answer is simple: none of you. For I serve an even higher power."

From his nostrils formed thin grey tentacles that grew across his upper lip like a mustache. His eyes turned glass black. His mouth, shaped in a deadly V of worn teeth and blood red gums, tried to say something further, but Catherine shoved Colada into his belly so fast, so hard, that de Huerva was still standing when she drew the blade back out.

The men attacked, and Catherine took three of them down before she was finally overwhelmed.

Someone stuck a boot in her face, and before she blacked out, Catherine heard Colada speak her name.

III

III

Fymurip awoke to a headache and six bodies swinging by the neck outside his hiding place. He blinked at least a dozen times to focus his bleary eyes on the surroundings. A lot of movement, talking, in both Spanish and in some language he could not decipher. It sounded Arabic, but he could not be sure. One thing was certain: those hanging by the neck weren't the ones talking.

He refocused on those bodies, and he realized now that he was in a cage, with iron bars, in the middle of a clearing. The bodies swung back and forth in the breeze and he watched them swing, losing sight of them briefly when they swung in front of the bars. It was almost dream-like, ethereal, and he tried to will himself awake. But he was already awake, and the bodies were real. He had seen worse in his days in Starybogow, and in the pit fights, but the starkness of their swinging, the simplicity of it, terrified him. It was almost like seeing fruit dangling from a tree.

"You should thank me," a voice behind his cage said. Fymurip jumped. "They had come to kill you."

He turned, and there stood Alfredo, his pasty green face covered in sweat. He'd been working hard on something. Then Fymurip saw the bloody dagger in his hand. "Who are they?"

Alfredo looked up briefly at the closest swinging body. "The Inquisition, of course. They came for you last night. Luckily, we were given word as to your whereabouts. We arrived just before they did. Lucky for you."

Fymurip looked at the bodies again, and it became clear. Their official clothing had eluded him in his dizziness. Alfredo continued, "But yes, they were de Deza's goons, and if they had caught you, they would have returned you to Zaragoza and the Queen."

Fymurip shook his head. "Isabella let us go."

Alfredo nodded. "Let you go... or let you escape so as to be caught again? Everybody, even queens, have their own role to play in this battle between Christianity and Islam, and the Eldar gods want to ensure that it comes out in the manner that best suits their objectives. And you, my good friend, will play a most important role. You and your lady love."

Fymurip spit through the bars towards Alfredo. The little creature stepped back a pace. "If you have harmed Catherine in any way—"

"So it is true," Alfredo said, his face contorting in a devilish grin. "You do love her. I was not certain. But it's understandable. Lady Catherine is quite the little dervish, isn't she? And if I were a man—ah, but none of that now. Now, we await your lady love."

"Where is she?"

Alfredo closed his eyes. For a moment, Fymurip thought the creature had fallen asleep. Then he opened them, and said, "She's here."

Fymurip heard her voice before he saw her. She was cursing in Spanish. He'd heard her do that before. But there was an anger, a violence in her voice this time that scared him almost as much as the bodies swinging in the trees above his head.

Then a line of men appeared across the clearing. Between them they carried a cage, like his own, and inside was Catherine, clutching the bars and screaming at them with every breath. But as he had heard on their approach, her voice was hoarse, scratchy. She had been screaming at them for a long time. But there was something else. She was terrified. She was crying as she screamed; he could hear that now. Fymurip reached out to his own bars, clutched them hard, and pulled himself against the front of his cage. Catherine...

They brought Catherine into the clearing and set her cage down, about thirty feet from Fymurip's. They faced each other, but it took a moment for Catherine to get her bearings and realize where she was and who was in the cage in front of her.

"Fymurip!"

Hearing her shout his name was the sweetest thing he had ever heard, and he tried calling back. A voice behind him, one he did not recognize, interrupted him.

"We must have a demonstration."

Fymurip turned, and there stood a man next to Alfredo. He was tall, thin, his olive-colored skin giving away his heritage. He was not a local; that was certain. Arabic? Moor? Perhaps. He towered over Alfredo, his eyes wild with excitement, and fear.

"It is risky," Alfredo said. "They are not in the arena. There is little security here."

"I cannot go back to my masters with hollow gifts, Alfredo." His accent was clear now. He was an Arab. But from where? "I must see the proof with my own eyes."

Alfredo baulked, then relented. He nodded. "Very well, but if this goes badly..."

"The blame rests with me," the man said.

Alfredo jumped onto Fymurip's cage, and Fymurip thought about reaching up and grabbing him. But the little Trasgo clapped his hands quickly, then jumped off.

Two men emerged from the tree line, each bearing a sword. They walked into the clearing between the cages. One of the men stepped a few paces in front of Fymurip's cage and laid Tizona onto the ground, its blade pointing at Catherine's cage. The other man did similar in front of Catherine's cage, but with a blade Fymurip had never seen before.

Colada.

It must be, and it was a beautiful blade, as much as he could see of it.

Alfredo appeared in front of Fymurip. He leaned over and put his face through the bars. "Now, you will fight."

Fymuip shook his head. "Never. I will never fight her."

"You will... or she will die. Open the cages!"

Was he bluffing? Creatures of Alfredo's ilk often lied to deceive, to get what they wanted. But the cages were opened, and their doors swung wide.

As much as he wanted to leap out and rush to Catherine, he paused, for the sword in front of him, again, spoke his name. "Fymurip Fymurip Fymurip..." replacing the incessant call for Colada. And why? Why now did Tizona call for him instead of Colada, as it had done so for weeks?

He had little time to contemplate the change, however, as anger and hatred grew in his mind. With each call of his name, Fymurip felt more anger, more hatred. More than he had ever felt before. But it wasn't pointed towards his captors, towards Alfredo, or the dead men swinging in the trees. It was pointed towards Catherine. Suddenly she was the object of this newfound hate, anger. Her lovely face turned dark, brooding. Her dark hair was suddenly knotted, unkempt, dirty. Suddenly she was the object of years and years of pent up anger toward Europe, towards Christians, that he had felt for a long, long time, but had never admitted. And he wanted her dead, so dead, like those men swinging above. With each call of his name, Fymurip slowly began to understand what he must do.

And like a dog, he leaped out of his cage towards Tizona.

*****

Catherine heard her name spoken over and over by the blade in front of her. "Catherine Catherine Catherine," and she could not resist. Where once before her, in the opposing cage, there was a man that she had grown to love, to respect, to value not simply as a companion, but as a human being, now she felt nothing but anger, rage in his presence. A Saracen, here, in my own country. What rights does he have... and though she tried fighting against those feelings, they would not subside. The only way to stop feeling this way, she realized, was to... was to...

She leaped from her cage, scooped up Colada in both hands, and charged Fymurip.

But he had done the same with Tizona, and in the middle, they met, their swords striking with a mighty spark. It was clear immediately that the Saracen was not comfortable using just one blade. He faltered after the first strike, fell back against Catherine's powerful swings of Colada. She nicked his arm. Then he twisted, rolled left, and came up beside her. She swung Colada again, but this time, he was ready. He blocked and counter stabbed, blocked and stabbed, such that she could not contain his attack. She fell back herself, capable only of blocking his relentless assault. Then she heard a voice. Not her own, and not even Colada's. A warrior's voice, the words in Spanish, but older Spanish. The dialect was not quite what she was used to, but it instructed her to move right, to feign falling, to let her enemy overcommit, and then to strike. She did so following the direction closely, and it all happened as she was directed. She fell back, she feigned falling, and the Saracen fell into her trap. She had him now. All it would take was one powerful swing towards his neck, and...

A dozen hands pulled her back, held her down. She struggled against them. She broke free for a moment, and Colada and Tizona clashed once more. Then they jumped on her and pressed her into the soft ground. They ripped open her hand and pulled Colada from her grip. She screamed, she struggled, but their weight was too much. They had her.

A few minutes later, her anger began to subside. Her heart stopped racing; her breathing returned to normal. They lifted her up and dragged her back to her cage. She watched Fymurip being dragged back to his. She looked at him with sensitive, caring eyes. He was no longer a Saracen. In her mind, he was back to being Fymurip, and she was thankful for that. She hoped that she would never feel that way about him again.

"Keep that sword away from me," she said as they threw her back into her cage. "It's cursed."

"Yes," Alfredo said to her as the cage door was shut and locked behind her. "But you put on a good show, and you proved what I had suspected for a long time."

Catherine wiped some blood from her mouth. Her cheek was sore. In the chaos of fighting Fymurip, he must have struck her mouth. "Yes, and what is that?"

"That you and your lover boy will prove a most valuable asset in the war that's coming." Alfredo nodded, clapped his hands again, and said, "Get them ready for travel. We leave within the hour."

"Where are we going?" Catherine asked.

Alfredo turned to her, smiled. "To Egypt, and there, my Lady Catherine, I assure you, the dragon will rise."

He left her, and Catherine turned to face Fymurip's cage. His face was pressed between the bars, his arm stretched out towards her. Catherine pressed her face between the bars and reached out to him. She wanted to speak, but all she could do was whisper his name over and over… "Fymurip Fymurip Fymurip…"

*****

May 1502 AD, Lübeck, in the German state of Schleswig-Holstein

Georg Cromer preferred sunlight over rain, but the gods never answered his prayers. In fact, most of the gods cared nothing about him, the good or bad ones. That was a comfort in a way, for in his line of work, drawing the attention of the gods usually ended in one's death. Perhaps he deserved death for the things he'd done in his life, but he hoped that today, in the midst of this incessant rain, the gods would shine upon him at least once.

The door to his office opened, and his assistant, Jacobus Knoblauch, entered. Georg turned to greet him, hoping to see a smile or a spring in the man's step. He got neither, and with a sigh, he asked, "What news from Spain?"

Jacobus pulled parchment from his pocket, and Georg waved him off. "Just tell me."

"They got Tizona, and they were on their way back to France."

"Yes?"

Jacobus hesitated, then, "But they were taken by her father back to Zaragoza, where, praise the Almighty, they managed to escape, although we're not entirely sure how. But..."

Georg crumpled his brow, annoyed with the hesitation. "Tell me!"

"She chose to go after Colada."

"Damn it all!"

Georg turned back to the window and the rain. He could hear thunder in the distance, see flashes of lightning over the dark spires of the city. "All we needed was one sword... one, and the Eldar Gods would have had little recourse but to face us here. Here, we could have set a trap to finish them once and for all. Impudent child! I warned her. She understood the danger of the situation, and she disobeyed me again. Now... it's over. The dragon will rise, Jacobus, and all the world will—"

"Perhaps, sir, the matter is not as dire as we fear."

Georg turned and lifted his brow. "How so?"

"Well, having two of the most powerful armies in the Holy Land tear each other apart could be for our benefit and for the benefit of Europe."

That was the prevailing philosophy of many in the Hanseatic League and in royal courts at large. A war there meant no war here. A war there meant a weakening of a counterforce against Christianity. If they weakened themselves overmuch, then Europe would simply start another crusade, and this time, there would be no stopping the Christian God and his armies. Georg shook his head in disbelief at the absurdity of the Idea; it was foolhardy at best, dangerous at worst. Did they not understand the nature of the Eldar gods, the nature of the threat? The Eldar gods did not care about land, property, industry, commerce. Nor did they care about benevolent gods more of the mind than of substance. No. They fed on chaos, and they fed well.

Georg turned, moved to his desk, and held out his hand. Jacobus gave him the parchment. Georg tucked it away for later. "Where is Catherine now?"

Jacobus shook his head. "We lost track of her in Madrid, I'm sorry to say, but most certainly she and her companion are heading to Egypt, if they aren't there already."

"And in the hands of Eldar cultists."

Jacobus nodded.

Georg pulled out his chair and sat down. "We must do what we can to salvage this mission, Jacobus. So do what you must. Send your best to Cairo, whether it be man, woman, or beast. Send them, and collect those swords if you can, find that impetuous little lady for sure... and bring her to me."

Part Four

The Fires of Egypt

I

Catherine awoke to a sore neck and her soiled clothing smelling of sweat and other foul things. Being confined to a small cage was enough to drive a person mad, and she certainly was mad. Not insane, but angry, enraged. Over and over in her mind, she imagined various way to kill Alfredo, and each more hideous and gruesome than the last. The one she liked the most was taking Fymurip's dagger and cutting the little beast's eyes out, one at a time, and listening to the screams as if they were sweet notes from the mouths of singing monks. But then the memory of monks reminded her of Bartolome, and her anger grew even stronger. She was thankful to God that she had had the opportunity to end that traitor's life before leaving Madrid. Every once in a while, the gods gave her a favor.

The rough wool quilt wrapped around her cage had blown aside, and now Catherine could see where she was. On a small, flat raft, being poled down a river by a man whose skin was lighter than she would have imagined, given their location. They were in Egypt; that was certain. She had never been here before, but the stories she'd heard as a child from travelling merchants and priests, spreading the word of God, gave her enough reference to know. They were on the Nile. Where they were headed, specifically, she did not know, but the heat, the dry air, the rough foliage along the banks, the crocodiles, were undeniable.

They were in the land of the Pharaohs.

The trip across the Mediterranean had been shorter than she had imagined. Curled into a painful ball, she fell into a fitful sleep, and when she awoke, she and her little cage were being hoisted off the ship and placed into a caravan. And now here she was, on a raft, heading down the Nile. Thankfully, she wasn't alone.

Fymurip's cage was tucked underneath a pile of crates, sacks, and barrels about ten feet away, but she could see enough of him to know that he was well. Alive, at least, and under the circumstances, that was enough. She hadn't spoken to him since they had left Madrid, and there was so much she wanted to say to him, so much she wanted to confess. But not here, not right now. Hopefully, there would be time for such discussion after whatever it was waiting for them. If they survived.

The thought of dying had never really occurred to Catherine. She'd been all over Europe, done so many dangerous, reckless things. She should have already been dead many times over. But contemplating death was something that less skilled, less capable people did. Now, she thought of very little else. She had underestimated the Eldar threat in Spain, but if she survived Egypt, she promised herself to always be careful, cautious, and never ever disrespect the enemy again.

"You look like you're in deep thought, my Lady."

Alfredo's voice was easily recognizable. She had heard it over and over in her mind since leaving Spain. Catherine looked around her cage, hoping that she'd find the little cretin beside her. No such luck. It would have been most satisfying to grab his neck and bash his head against the iron bars. All she could see of him was his dark shadow on the quilt.

"I will kill you, Alfredo," Catherine hissed, "outright, if I ever get the chance."

"You should not be so angry with me, for I am the one who has saved you from the men we travel with. Many nights they have desired to touch you. I've kept them from acting on their worst inclinations. So, you see, fair Catherine, I still serve you."

"You serve me by bringing me to my death?"

She could not see his face, but Catherine could tell Alfredo was smiling. "We'll see."

Something struck Afredo. He yelped and fell back. "Get away from her." It was Fymurip's voice.

Catherine's heart leapt and she scrambled forward and grabbed the iron bars of her cage. She pushed her face through as far as she could, hoping to see her companion out of his cage, armed with his blades. Alas, no. He was still confined like her. She sighed. "Fymurip... are you all right?"

"Well enough to cast a pebble, at least."

His face was dirty and rough with black stubble, but his eyes were as radiant as they had ever been. "Where are they taking us?" Catherine asked.

"To Cairo, I would imagine. Into the city of the slave kings."

Catherine shook her head. "I don't understand."

"The Mamluks. The Burji Mamluks, to be exact. They rule Egypt now."

"How do you know so much? You've never been here."

It looked as though Fymurip smiled, and perhaps chuckled a little. It was difficult for her to tell through the bars. "You're right, I haven't. But when you serve the Sultan, you hear a lot about their enemies."

"Did you ever fight against the Mamluks?" Catherine asked.

"No, never, Praise Allah, or you and I might never have met. I served Sultan Beyazid II as part of a Tatar cavalry regiment assigned primarily to Wallachia and Hungary; that is why I found myself so easily in Eastern Prussia and not somewhere in the Levant. Remember: the Mamluk army stopped the Mongol horde from sweeping through Africa and, probably, into Spain. The stories of those triumphs are known across the world."

A crewman stepped between them, paused a moment, then moved on. Catherine followed him with her eyes, then said, "They're so white, these Mamluks. Why?"

Again, Fymurip chuckled. "I promise, someday, I will tell you as much as I know about Egypt, Arabia, Persia, and anywhere else you wish to know about. But for now, know that the Burjis are not Arabic. They are Circassian. They are, in essence, Russians from the Black Sea. Not very far from where I was born, in truth. I suppose I have more in common with them than I do with the Turks."

"How did they get all the way down here?"

"'Mamluk', Catherine, means slave in Arabic. These men were slaves, taken from the Black Sea area and made soldiers. Or rather, they are the descendants of those slave soldiers, men who broke free from their bonds and formed one of the most powerful Caliphates the world has ever seen. Well, most powerful once. Now... I'm not so sure. The years have not been so kind to the Mamluks."

"And is that why we have been brought here? To help them become strong again?"

"Us? No. We are not that important, you and I, in whatever plans they have. But Tizona, Colada, they are important. I'm sure of that."

"Then why keep us? Why? They have what they want. Why not let us go?"

"I don't know. That is the part which alludes me, but I'm sure it has something to do with our fight."

Catherine paused a moment, then, "I'm sorry, Fymurip. I'm sorry for how I went after you."

Fymurip nodded. "Me too. We were not ourselves. I would no more draw blades against you than my own mother, my sister."

"Is that was you think of me? As a sister?"

She regretted the question the moment she asked it. Now was not the time for such talk, but she was tired—exhausted, in fact—afraid, and she needed to know his thoughts, his feelings.

The wool quilt was pulled back over her cage before Fymurip answered.

Catherine did not call again for him to answer. She turned away from the bars, rolled up into her ball, and tried not to cry.

*****

Her question weighed heavily on his mind. Of course, you are not my sister… don't be silly. That might have been his response had he been given a chance. You are more, much more. But the words did not come, even though he could have spoken them through the wool blanket secured around her cage. He just didn't have the courage to answer.

A few hours later, the raft pulled up to a dock, and both cages were hoisted out and onto solid ground. Fymurip was thankful for that. Though the Nile was relatively shallow, and its waves were minor compared to the Mediterranean Sea, he was still tired of rocking and sloshing around. Especially in his filthy state. Allah, did he need a bath! He did not even want to be near Catherine now, no matter how much he cared for her, for surely she would vomit if she could smell him.

They were carried this time, like palanquins, with poles stuck through the bars. Both Circassian Mamluks and traditional Egyptian Muslims carried them, and the farther they travelled down the narrow and sandy path, the louder and more crowded did the roads become. Then they crested a hill, and there it lay: *Cairo*.

Fymurip marveled at its size, it sprawling beauty, its utter mass of humanity that wavered back and forth through ancient structures of stark stone and clay, and for the first time in over a year, he could hear people speak Arabic as freely as they breathed. And just like when he was in the bazaar in Constantinople, he felt at home.

The men carrying their cages were given orders from Alfredo to move faster. He bounced ahead of the caravan, trying to avoid the powerful strides of several camels that cared little about his authority. One even spit at the little Trasgo, and too bad that it missed. If he were close to the cage, Fymurip might have tried to do the same.

Down into the morass of people were they carried, and despite the ominous appearance that their caravan held—the well-equipped guards, wielding sharp swords and spears, that walked along with them—people gathered all around and pushed up to their cages. Children reached in to try and touch Fymurip. He ignored them, though he did try to smile at them to ensure their curious little minds that he was not a threat. Most were far more interested in Catherine, for it was rare to see a European woman in their midst. Most had probably never seen one, and many of the little girls reached in to try and touch her hair. Fymurip wished that he could reach in and touch her hair and stroke her head and let her know that it would be all right. But then, he wasn't sure of that himself.

They were taken far into the city, and then Alfredo ordered them to be set down in the middle of a bazaar. No, not a bazaar like the one he remembered in Constantinople. This one was different: a bazaar where only knives and spears and shields and handguns and crossbows and armor were being made and bartered and sold. Fymurip had only see one of these kinds of bazaars in all his life.

"They're going to war."

"Who?" Catherine asked. Her cage had been set down right beside his.

"The Mamluks."

"Against who?"

Before he could answer, the large clump of citizens that had gathered to stare divided, and another palanquin arrived. The guards lining its path for its protection were far more impressive and heavily armed, wearing thick leather armor, iron helmets, and mail aventails. The crowd gave a wide berth as the palanquin was brought into the center of the bazaar and placed down about twenty feet in front of Fymurip's cage.

Someone clapped twice, and the iron locks and chains on their cages were removed. Fymurip was hastened out by a long, hairy arm. He stretched his legs and slowly crawled out.

The hot, afternoon sun blinded him for a moment, but soon his vision returned. He stood erect, holding himself straight and proud, not allowing the men around him to see an ounce of weakness. Catherine, poor girl, was not so inclined.

She crawled out of the cage, and it took two men to bring her to her feet. Eventually, she was able to stand on her own, though she leaned a little to the right. Fymurip reached out and caught her before she fell. Surprisingly, the guards allowed them to touch. Fymurip was glad. Despite their dishevelment, it felt good to be so near to her.

The crowd was brought to silence. The palanquin door opened, and out stepped a short, but solid, man dressed in the finest clothing.

The man's turban was yellow with a red brim. The cloth that hung from the turban, which protected his neck from the blazing sun, was also yellow with a red flowing pattern of ornate flowers. His robes were elegant, though simple, more of a shift than a full-fledged royal robe. Over his shoulders hung a red cape which unraveled to his feet, which were covered in fresh leather slippers.

Everyone bowed as he walked forward towards Fymurip. Despite the anger in his heart, Fymurip bowed as well, helping Catherine do the same.

Alfredo stepped forward with the man, a wide grin across his face. "I brought them to you, Your Majesty, as I have promised. I brought them—"

The man backhanded the Trasgo so hard that blood and a tooth burst from Alfredo's mouth as he flew through the air and struck the ground several feet away.

Not missing a step, the man collected himself, walked up to Fymurip and Catherine, and paused.

"I greet you warmly," he said, bowing slightly. "I am Al Ashraf Qansur al Ghuri, Sultan of the Burji Dynasty. I welcome you both to Egypt and to Cairo."

II

Sultan al Ghuri's salutation was so pleasant that, under better circumstances, Fymurip might have responded in kind. But he wasn't in the mood for pleasant talk. "I appreciate your treatment of Alfredo, Your Majesty, but we have been brought here against our will and under duress. I demand that we be released immediately."

The sultan, nonplussed at the demand, leaned forward, sniffed the air, and blanched. He turned to stare at Alfredo, who was searching the sand and gravel for his lost tooth. "You filthy pig! Have you no decency? Bringing these people to us in such a state. Clean them," he ordered a servant nearby, "and give them new clothing, and food.

"I apologize for your harsh treatment," he said to Catherine. "Such treatment of a royal daughter is beneath contempt. Go now, and refresh yourselves, and then we shall talk. And I will gladly explain everything."

"My swords. Where are my swords?" Fymurip asked as they were being shuffled away.

Al Ghuri shook his head. "I do not know, but the only swords that should matter to you now are Tizona and Colada. Take them away."

They were removed from the Sultan's presence and taken to a small bathhouse near what Fymurip assumed was al Ghuri's royal palace, though the structure looked old, disheveled. Perhaps it had once housed the great Pharaohs, or some Ptolemaic or Roman ruler. Perhaps Cleopatra herself had walked the hallway down which they were being led. If time were convenient, Fymurip might have enjoyed exploring the palace and Cairo itself. So much important Middle Eastern history resided in Egypt; it would be a shame to let the opportunity go to waste. But the men handling him were not concerned about such things. He and Catherine were separated and taken in different directions.

He was ushered into a room with a bath of steaming water. There, as in Constantinople, he was greeted by slave girls (Berbers perhaps) that unrobed him and then took their sweet time, scrubbing away every speck of dirt from his skin. And like Constantinople, he let them work, though this time, he was less enthusiastic to let them stray from their appointed duty. Now was not the time for such play, and besides, allowing these women to satisfy him physically seemed like a betrayal of Catherine. Fymurip could not believe that he felt that way, for he had never felt that way about anyone in his life. Oh, how times had changed.

When they finished, he was dressed in red pantaloons, white shirt, and yellow vest. A pair of slippers were offered. Fymurip accepted them grudgingly, for it felt good not having anything on his sore, calloused feet, but he put them on anyway and waited. And waited. And waited. It seemed as if they were content to let him wither away in the humid air of the tightly closed bath.

Then the doors opened, and three men entered. They were not the guards that had handled him earlier. These men were larger, stronger, and Fymurip did not resist their instruction to follow. They did not lay hands on him; that was a comfort, for he was tired of being grabbed and pushed and prodded. They let him follow, two in front, one behind. He followed them through the rest of the bathhouse, through a mosque, and into the palace proper, where in a long, rectangular room, stood a table.

Catherine was already there, sitting at the far end, up near the head of the table where a small, though opulent, throne sat empty. Like him, she had been bathed and given new clothing. Fymurip was surprised, however, that she was not dressed in traditional Mamluk female garb. She was in very much the same type of clothing that he wore: loose, comfortable, allowing the wearer great flexibility.

Fymurip was taken to the other side of the table where they placed him in a chair opposite Catherine. They stared at each other, though Catherine's eyes kept wandering to the feast in between. Dates and cherries, melons, almonds, stewed meats, hummus, flat bread, and even some Turkish dishes that Fymurip recognized. There was wine and water and a broth of some kind. The smells were intoxicating, and Fymurip had to keep his hands to his sides and his mouth from watering.

"You look nice," he said to Catherine.

"What?"

Fymurip didn't know if she asked because she did not hear, or if she could not believe her ears. He shook his head, making light of it. "Nothing. Never mind."

In time, al Ghuri entered with his personal guard. Behind them followed Alfredo sporting a swollen face and a weary look. Behind him were two men with their arms held out and draped in a fine red silk. On the silk lay Tizona and Colada. Fymurip could hear their call to one another even across the room.

Al Ghuri took his throne. The men carrying the swords laid them in the center of the table, away from the food. Then they nodded to their Sultan and left. The Sultan's personal guard stepped back and covered the two doorways. Alfredo seemed afraid to take a chair at first, but al Ghuri nodded, and the little Trasgo hopped up.

"Eat," the Sultan said. "There is plenty, and I am sure you are famished."

Catherine wasted no time digging in, taking a piece of flat bread and dipping it generously into the hummus. Fymurip chose a few dates and ladled out some of the stew. He considered the wine, but instead poured water into his goblet. Alfredo seemed hesitant at first, but then picked a few almonds and nearly swallowed them whole.

It went on like this for a while, everyone stuffing their faces, except for the Sultan himself, who sat their contently, patiently, a wry smile on his face.

When everyone had reached a point where their feasting had slowed, al Ghuri spoke. "I am glad to see you both well, though you may be surprised at that sentiment, given the fact that I have, as you say, brought you here against your will. It is important to me that you both are healthy and strong."

"Why?" Catherine asked as she swallowed down a final bit of date.

"Because Lady Catherine, you and your Tatar companion will help me destroy the Turkish army."

*****

"And why would we do that?"

Fymurip's question was valid. Catherine wished that she had asked it herself, but she was determined to drink some of that wine before it went to waste. She took a sip. She closed her eyes. It was strong, but oh so delicious.

"Because, Fymurip Azat," al Ghuri said, "Sultan Beyazid II is intent on destroying me and my Caliphate. He longs to walk the

Nile of the great Pharaohs, for he believes that Egypt is the soul of the Middle East. And he is not wrong about that. But we must not allow him to acquire it, for if we do, could Europe, could Spain, be far behind?"

Catherine huffed and set down her goblet. She wiped her wet mouth with the back of her hand. "You want me to believe that you have my country's best interests at heart? I'm young, Your Majesty, and perhaps I'm just a girl in your eyes, but I am no fool."

"Nor did I take you for one," al Ghuri said. He nodded towards Alfredo. "That little cretin has told me all about you, and though not a word he speaks can be trusted, I believe what he says about King Ferdinand's daughter. But in your heart, you must know that what I am saying is true. If the Turks get hold of Egypt, why would they be content to stop? Like the Moors, they will look jealously upon your shores, and there will they send their finest to kill and rape and pillage until all of Europe lays in ashes. They have made several attempts at Europe already, through Wallachia, Romania, Hungary. They have not been entirely successful there, yet I will concede, but Egypt is not the high spires of the Carpathian Mountains. There is only a small waterway between Africa and Iberia, Catherine of Aragon. Do not think for a moment that you are safe from another invasion because your father, your mother, vanquished a minor Caliphate whose time had come to an end. I am speaking truth. You know that I am."

"With respect, Your Majesty," Fymurip said before Catherine had a chance to respond. "How do you intend on defeating what could be the most powerful army in the world? I have fought against them. I have fought with them. Their ranks count in the thousands. Akinji light cavalry. Sipahi heavy cavalry. Azabs and Dervishes. Dellis cavalry and provincial forces that number in the tens of thousands. And do not forget the Janissary, Your Majesty. And cannon and jinns and efreets and scores of other creatures swell their ranks to bursting. I have seen them in action, and it terrifies me to imagine what devilment awaits your army if you choose to meet them in open battle. The Mamluk Caliphate once housed a great army. Your people stopped the Mongol Horde in its tracks, and for that, even I am grateful. But not anymore. Those days are long, long gone. How can you hope to defeat them now?"

Al Ghuri's eyes glazed over as if Fymurip's words had hurt him deeply. Catherine paused, waiting for the Sultan to speak, and she followed his eyes as they gazed upon the swords laying on the table. Al Ghuri lifted a heavy hand and pointed at the blades. "They will help me defeat the Turks. Won't they, Catherine?"

The Sultan, Fymurip, even Alfredo, stared at her. For a moment, she felt self-conscious, as if there was something wrong with her face. But al Ghuri's question was clear, and she knew the answer, though she could not believe it.

El dragon hay que levantarse.

"The dragon will rise... What does that mean, Catherine?" Fymurip asked, his eyes wide, his expression lost, confused.

She had told him all that she knew about the swords and their history after they had escaped Zaragoza. She had told him only the facts as she understood them. She failed to mention her suspicions, for what good were suspicions anyway when they were going to find Colada and be back in Germany within a month? Such suspicions would be useless to dwell on under those circumstances, and so, why speak them?

"I'm sorry, I—"

"She deceived you, Fymurip." Al Ghuri's deep laugh raked her spine like fingernails. "She knows more, or has suspected more, than she has confessed." He turned his attention to her. "You should have left Spain with Tizona alone. You were deceived as well, by your mother, your priest, by this little cretin with an almond stuck in the gap of his missing tooth. You only needed Tizona, Catherine, as the League requested. But you second-guessed your superiors in Lübeck and yourself. And for that, I'm infinitely grateful. And now, Fymurip Azat, you will learn what *el dragon hay que levantarse* means."

Al Ghuri clapped thrice, and the men guarding the doors seized Catherine. Fymurip fought his guards, crushing one of their throats with a strong jab to the neck, but he was overpowered and brought under control.

Tizona and Colada were taken as well, the doors thrown open, and out into the street they were dragged. Civilians lined their route, cheering, waving palm fronds, smiling, singing. It was not the reception Catherine expected, for how could these people rejoice in what was coming?

What was coming? Even now, she could not imagine it, could not even think it. The idea was so outrageous, so impossible, it had to be false, and yet, here they were. Whether it was true or not, these Mamluks thought it was true, and they were intent on making it happen.

They rounded a corner, and high above the stone and brick buildings along their path, rose the oval shape of an arena.

III

III

Fymurip took in the sight of the arena with a dread that he hadn't felt since confronting the Vucari in Starybogow. The arena itself was a Roman structure; it had to be. He had never visited Italy, had never seen the famed Colosseum, but this structure was too similar to the tales he'd been told of that wondrous architecture. Smaller, yes, but still capable of holding thousands of spectators.

"Open the gate!" One of their guards barked, and they were ushered through the gate and into the center of the arena.

As they entered, the crowd erupted with cheers, shouts, and ululations of the tongue. Not a seat was empty, and the arena rocked with the stamping of feet. Some threw bouquets of flowers; others, pieces of cloth tied around stones or pebbles. Fymurip could not tell which, but they had a weight to them that caused them to strike the arena ground and remain fixed. Perhaps they were filled with sand. He stepped over them and continued.

They were halted in the middle of the arena, and Tizona and Colada were brought forward. Tizona was placed on the ground a few feet from Fymurip; Colada was set near Catherine. Just like in Madrid before they were caged and brought here. Fymurip's heart sank, for the incessant call of Tizona to Colada changed as it did in Madrid. "Fymurip Fymurip Fymurip" it said over and over. He shook his head, covered his ears, trying to ignore the swelling desire in his mind.

"No!" He shouted. "I will not pick up the sword. I will not fight!"

He turned towards the door, took three steps, and a rush of arrows struck the ground before him, one missing his leg by inches. He looked up into the crowd; men with composite bows were scattered throughout the stands, and they were preparing another volley. Fymurip pulled one of the arrows out of the sand, broke it against his knee, and cast it aside. "What do you want from us?"

"We want you to fight!"

Al Ghuri's voice echoed across the arena. Fymurip looked up again and saw the Sultan standing just above the gate. "You will fight, to the death if necessary, or I promise… you will die."

Another volley of arrows struck the ground near his feet.

Fymurip stepped back, shook his head. "I would rather die than fight her."

But even as he said it, he saw the shadow of someone approaching grow long across the ground, and he turned just in time to duck a sword swing from Catherine.

In her tight grip lay Colada, and her eyes were glazed over, much like the Sultan's had been in the dining hall, and it was clear to him that she meant to strike him and strike hard, whether she wanted to or not.

He rolled away from another swing, gained his feet, and ran to pick up Tizona.

It felt good in his hands, like it had before, and the sword stopped calling his name, as if by touching it, it was home. Fymurip felt the rush of contentment first, and then rage. Rage against the woman that came at him again, her teeth bared, her will fixed on fighting him, and yes, to the death if necessary.

He raised Tizona and blocked her swing. The swords met in a clamber that hurt his ears. And she was relentless, striking again and again and again, driving him back until he was near flush against the arena wall. Then he lowered the sword, just a little, to give her the belief that he was tiring. She took the bait, like many of his opponents had done in the pit fights around Starybogow. She swung too high. He ducked. Her blade struck the arena wall in a shower of sparks. She screamed and tried to recover, but her balance was off. Fymurip lunged at her chest, took her in a tight hug, and brought her to the ground.

But Colada had given her strength, and she simply rolled with the tackle, put her knees into his stomach, and flipped him aside. She was up again, standing over him, before he even recovered.

Fymurip rolled twice as Catherine tried to bring her foot down onto his throat. He then used Tizona's hilt to strike her knee. Catherine screamed, fell back, giving him time to rise and recover, and to marvel at the speed through which Catherine conducted her assault. He was impressed, but no amount of energy and strength given to her through Colada would keep her wielding it like a dervish for long. She was tiring; he could see it in how low she held the sword, how the blade tipped forward a few more inches than it had when they had started. In truth, the sword was just too large for her, too heavy, and she was trying to compensate by speed and guile. It had succeeded so far, but how much longer could she go on?

He wanted to tell her to throw down her sword, to give up. He wanted to do the same, but he just could not drop it. Whatever strength Colada gave to Catherine, whatever had possessed it in the first place, was also possessing him. He tried opening his hands and letting Tizona drop to the ground, but he could not do it. And Catherine attacked and attacked and attacked. And as she did, he grew angrier and more annoyed that she would not stop. He knew that it was not her fault, but that did not seem to matter. The love that he had felt just moments ago for this swirling dark-headed dervish had turned dark, sour. All he thought of now was to stop her attack, and if it meant killing her...

The gates of the arena opened, and in streamed the elite guard of the Sultan, men in full chain, red capes, with iron helmets, shields and spears. Dozens of them, and they did not stop entering until they had created a full circle surrounding the center of the arena. Behind them entered five men in black robes, carrying nets and ropes with hooks. Their hoods were pulled forward so that their faces could not be seen, but in the shadow of those hoods, Fymurip could see their red glowing eyes.

Eldar cultists.

Then it all made sense to him, everything. All the moving pieces fell into place.

He tried to speak, to tell Catherine to stop fighting, to not give them what they wanted, but his words caught in his throat. It was as if he could not speak at all. Something was keeping his mouth from forming the words that he tried screaming at Catherine across the bloody space between them. The words he heard in his mind, instead, were "Kill her! Kill her now!"

He attacked, with the fury and speed that he had perfected in the pit fights. And she was good, very good, blocking blow after blow. But she was spent, near the end. She could not block every swipe, every thrust. First, her arm took a nick. Then her shoulder. Then her face. Small cuts, yes, but in total, they could be deadly. Fymurip tried holding back, tried fighting against the command in his mind to bring her down. And he could see the desperation on her face, her eyes wide with fear. She could not stop him, and Fymurip had no intention of stopping, until she lay dead on the ground.

She stumbled and lay flat, holding Colada up to block Fymurip's next attack.

He moved in for the kill.

*****

Catherine fought against the voice in her mind that told her to attack, attack, attack, and give no quarter to this "Saracen" before her. But he was strong, so strong, too strong in fact for her weakening arms. Colada was too big, too unwieldy for her strength. Yet she had used it well against her enemy... no, not her enemy. Fymurip. The man that she had travelled with for nearly a year, the man that stood before her now, his relentless counterattack pushing her to her back. This was a man she loved, more so than perhaps she would admit to herself. But the voice in her mind kept breaking him down into his basic parts: foreign, Tatar, Saracen, Muslim. And somehow the voice in her mind had convinced her that Fymurip was an offense to her, to her family, to every Christian thing she had stood for. No... no! She would not give in to such hate, to such blind anger.

Fymurip came at her again. She held her sword up, gripping Colada's handle with one hand, the end of the blade with the other, despite the pain she felt as the blade cut into her fingers. She held it up, locking her elbows so that her waning strength would not give out. She screamed as Fymurip swung Tizona down.

The swords met with a mighty spark. The blow rocked Catherine's body, but she held Colada strong as Tizona struck it square... and shattered.

Then Colada shattered, and suddenly, Catherine was able to release the hilt and crawl away.

Between her and Fymurip, the swords continued to crack, and crack, and crack, until powerful white light streamed out of the cracks. Catherine covered her eyes from the blinding light. The crowd fell silent, and the elite guard which had come into the arena stepped forward slowly, closing the circle on their position.

Catherine crawled further away but dared to look back at El Cid's swords that lay on the arena sand, splintering and cracking and popping with light and smoke. The smoke swirled up into the air like a funnel, and a voice roared from the broken swords. Not a voice really, but a demonic shout, then a high-pitched screech that sent a chill down Catherine's spine. For she knew now what that screech meant; the stories she had heard, the rumors, were all true.

The dragon was rising.

"Run!" She managed to scream to Fymurip who sat on the other side of the swords. "Run!"

She turned and ran, and surprisingly, the guards parted and let her run. But she could not escape the arena, though she moved as far away from the breaking swords as she could.

Fymurip joined her, and she wrapped her bloody arms around him as tight as the grip he had given her on his tackle a moment ago. "I'm sorry," she said, rubbing the back of his head, showering his rough, dirty face with kisses. "I'm so sorry."

He kissed and hugged her back. "No, do not worry about it. I've got you... I've got you."

Behind them, the swords erupted into the sky.

Shards of steel blew upward like a cloud, and from their source, rose *Cuélebre*.

It was the most massive creature Catherine had ever seen. It even dwarfed the Eldar God which had come partially through the portal at Starybogow, for this beast was thicker, wider, and its arms and legs were roped with steel-like muscle. Its scales were red and black, and as it grew into its full size, it stretched its long neck over the guards that now held their spears and shields forward. It opened its eyes, blinked several times, ran its black tongue over newly formed sharp white teeth. It seemed to belch, as if it were trying to throw up a gout of blood. It arched its back, fluttered out its bat-like wings, raised itself up on strong hind legs, and let fly a line of fire from its maw that cut through the guards and ripped through the crowd.

Such horrible screams of men, women, and children Catherine had never heard. Fymurip tried to shield her eyes from the horror unfolding within the crowd, but she could not look away, for she blamed herself for their deaths. This was her fault. She had foolishly gone after Colada, bringing both swords together, and now innocent people burned. My fault... all my fault.

The shaking guards moved forward to close up on the dragon, and the Eldar cultists moved even closer, shouting their incantations, waving their arms, dancing their dances, all in an attempt to bring the beast under control. But *Cuélebre* let out another line of fire that struck the crowd, though this time, not so many died, as the people were running for their lives. Enough burned, however, to make Catherine cry.

She lay there in Fymurip's arms, such strong arms holding her tightly, his gentle hand stroking her head. He sang a song to her in Arabic. She did not understand the words, but they soothed her. Enough, at least, for her to calm. And she closed her eyes as the Eldar cultists continued to work on controlling the dragon.

She slept, for how long, she did not know. When she awoke, she and Fymurip were still in the arena, but everyone else, including *Cuélebre*, was gone.

IV

It was dark, save for a few torches that burned along the circular wall of the arena. It was quiet, too quiet for Fymurip's pleasure, as if the entirety of Cairo had left en masse. Then somewhere in the distance, beyond the walls, *Cuélebre* roared. A muffled roar, indeed, but one that sent a chill down his spine. They were still in Cairo, still a "guest" of the Sultan al Ghuri, and the dragon had risen.

"Can you walk?" He asked Catherine.

She nodded. He felt her movement against his chest. He held her tight, stood slowly, and paused. "Are we still prisoners, I wonder?"

"I don't know," Catherine said, regaining her feet and strength. She pushed away from him, ran her hands through her mangled hair, sniffed a few times, and rubbed her eyes as if she were trying to rub them away. She cleared her throat. "Let's go."

"Where?"

Catherine shook her head. "I don't know, but away from here."

They walked, slowly, towards one of the two gates that led out of the arena. As they drew closer to the city, Fymurip could hear the rumble of voices, the patter of movement, from the outside street. Cairo was coming back alive to him, all the sounds, smells, the dry heat, everything. They walked through the gate, through the short hallway that led out of the arena, and into the Cairo sprawl.

They were ignored by passersby, as if they were just two more persons, non-descript, unimportant. There were no guards, no Mamluk soldiers to keep an eye on them to ensure they did not stray or cause trouble. It was both refreshing and, honestly, insulting. "That's it? That's all? We are nothing to them now? After all we've done?"

"What have we done, Fymurip?" Catherine asked as they slowly picked their way through the crowds. There was a twitch of anger on her lips. "We have delivered a dragon to al Ghuri. We have destroyed El Cid's swords. I, personally, have violated my oath and charge to the League. In the end, we may very well have delivered death and desolation to hundreds, thousands, of Turks, and tipped the balance of power in favor of the Mamluks. The last thing we deserve right now is attention."

"That's not what I meant," Fymurip said, annoyed. He was in no mood for an argument. "I'm just surprised that they would let us walk away with nothing, not even a nod, as if it was all a dream."

"Perhaps it was. Perhaps we are living in the mind of my sister Joanna, playing the part in one of her demented games. If not, then this is real, and as such, we will do best to keep our heads down, and make our way out. There is nothing more we can do."

The high, whiny chuckle came from their left. They paused, turned, and saw Alfredo standing there, knee high. He shook his head derisively. "You still do not understand the Eldar gods, do you, my Lady?"

Fymurip moved to seize the little Trasgo, but a large, very large, man stepped between them. He stood near seven feet, and his biceps were almost as large as Fymurip's head. He wore loose clothing, white pantaloons, a white shirt, and a red vest. His head was bare. His face was broad and covered with black whiskers. "Take caution, Fymurip," Alfredo said, "for my friend is not polite to those who threaten my person. I do not intend to ever lose another tooth."

"What don't I understand?" Catherine asked, moving forward to stand between Fymurip and Alfredo's bodyguard.

"That the Eldar gods thrive on chaos. Al Ghuri and the Mamluks do not care about the Eldar gods any more than they love or hate Islam, or Christianity, or any other religion that mortal man chooses to believe. He simply desires a weapon that he can throw against the Turks as they move through the Levant, on their way to Cairo. Al Ghuri just wants his Burji Dynasty to live another year, and another, and another."

"Then if the Mamluks do not care about the Eldar gods," Fymurip asked, "why have so many cultists, why have you, aligned yourself with them? Why not ally with the Turks? They are far more powerful than the Mamluks ever will be again."

"Ah," Alfredo said, raising a finger as if he had just remembered an important point, "therein lies the answer. Indeed, there are those within the Ottoman ranks that want to see the rise of the Eldar gods, and they work diligently for that end. And we work beside them in our capacity. But Sultan Bayezid's army is too powerful, too successful, and that kind of stability works against the Eldar gods.

The powers that are required to bring them into this world are best in the midst of chaos, in the middle of bloody, torturous war.

"If al Ghuri can wield *Cuélebre* long enough to drive the Turks out of the Levant and deliver to them tens of thousands of corpses, Bayezid's army will be weakened considerably, and the doorway between this world and the Eldar gods can be opened."

"Why are you telling us this?" Catherine asked. "Do you think we will help you ensure the destruction of the Turks? Why would we do that?"

"Notice, my Lady, that I used the words 'long enough.' Cuélebre must thrive only long enough to weaken the Turkish army, but not to destroy it, for if it is allowed to do that, then the Mamluks simply replace the Ottomans as the most power army in the world. And we are then put in the same position that we are in today."

Fymurip huffed. "All the more reason to walk away. Let al Ghuri and his *Cuélebre* destroy the Ottoman Empire, and then you and your filthy Eldar gods will have to find another way to enter."

Fymurip and Catherine turned to walk away. "Very well," said Alfredo, "you may choose to go and let matters play out as they will. But if Cuélebre is allowed to thrive, then I promise you, al Ghuri will turn his attention to Iberia, and all that you love, Lady Catherine - your mother, your sister, and yes, even your hateful father - will fall. The longer the dragon is allowed to endure, it will grow stronger, and stronger, and stronger, until all of Europe will burn in its fire."

"This is the same warning that al Ghuri gave us about the Turks," Catherine said, almost smirking.

Alfredo nodded. "And he was right. In either case, Europe is not equipped right now to endure an Ottoman or a Mamluk onslaught. Don't you understand, my Lady? Sultan al Ghuri and Sultan Bayezid must meet on a field of battle, and they must bloody one another such that Europe has time to reform, regroup, and raise an army itself strong enough to face any and all threats."

"You want us to believe that you have Europe's best interest at heart?" Fymurip asked.

Alfredo nodded. "Yes, I do. I am, regardless of my nature, Asturian." Alfredo turned to Catherine. "And I promised your mother that I would protect you, and I will, if you let me."

Fymurip sighed. The amount of scheming, the double-talk, from this cretin was beginning to make his head hurt. "You are confusing me, Alfredo. Regardless of how it plays out, in the end, if I understand you correctly, the Eldar gods will rise out of the chaos of war. Even if it plays out the way you say, in the end, Europe will fall to darkness."

"A lot can happen between now and then, Fymurip. Remember, your Teutonic friend is still out there, and he too has a role to play."

Lux Von Junker. With all that had happened, it had been a while since he had thought about his old friend. Where was he now? Fymurip wondered. In Cathay as promised, no doubt. And how did this sniveling little beast know about the knight anyway? Fymurip did not recall ever saying anything about him, though perhaps he had forgotten that as well. Or perhaps Alfredo, given his supernatural nature, knew things inherently. Fymurip sighed again. He looked at Catherine and wondered what she thought of all this. She did not speak. She simply stared back at him as if he knew the right decision to make.

So confusing…

"Very well," Fymurip said, taking a step towards Alfredo as he kept a wary eye on the Trasgo's bodyguard. "How can *Cuélebre* be vanquished? El Cid is dead, and his blades were destroyed. How can the dragon be stopped before it becomes too powerful?"

Alfredo smiled, clapped three times like al Ghuri had earlier. A smaller, thinner man stepped up, holding a leather bundle in his arms. He placed the bundle on the ground at Fymurip's feet and unraveled the bundle until its contents were revealed. Fymurip's eyes grew wide.

"You have two blades," Alfredo said, "and I know how to kill the dragon."

V

Catherine put her foot down. "No, you won't do it. I won't allow it. I am Catherine of Aragon, the daughter of the king and queen of Spain. Whatever authority I wield, I do so now. I refuse to let you go!"

His impulse was to shout back, "I'm not your slave," but that would be foolish. They had been through too much, and Catherine had always shown him great respect, and now, love. Fymurip could see the fear, the terror, in her eyes. Alfredo's idea was foolhardy, she was correct in that, but what other choice did they have? Either walk away... or fight.

"Then come with me," he said, setting his kilij sword and khanjar dagger correctly on his belt and hip. He felt whole again. "We can do this together."

"And die together? Is that how you want this to end?"

Fymurip sighed and took Catherine in his arms. He pulled her close. She melted into his chest. "No, I don't. But we've come this far. Do we really want to walk away empty-handed? Our actions, our foolish decisions, have released this monster on the world. Do we stop now, or do we try to right this great wrong? El Cid, *El Campeador*, would not have walked away."

Catherine sobbed against him. He could feel her wet face on his skin. "I know, but you are not Rodrigo Diaz de Vivar, Fymurip, as good as you are." She paused, then, "And I don't love him as I do you."

There it was, the words that he knew she had wanted to say for a long time. And he wanted to say them back, for he did feel the same way about her. In his bones, he knew it. But he needed to pray. He needed time to reflect on his feelings, to ask Allah for advice, to see more clearly a way forward for them to be together in a world that would, at best, shun their union. There had been instances where Christians and Muslims had come together as such in the past. The notion was not implausible. But in general, it was not acceptable. Did that matter? No, not to Fymurip specifically. What did he care if people unimportant to him did not approve of his relationship with Catherine? But the fact that she was royalty - and that could never be denied, no matter how much Catherine tried - made the issue complicated at best. And what of children? Where would they live? How would they be treated? And how would they be manipulated by forces yet unborn that would try to take advantage of their mixed blood, their mixed heritage? So many unanswered questions, so many mixed emotions, it was hard for him to keep them all clear.

But the matter at hand was paramount. *Cuélebre* mattered more than anything right now.

"Come with me," he said again, stroking her greasy hair. "Let's face this devil together, as we have faced all our devils to date. Together, we can be as strong as El Cid."

A moment more, and then Catherine nodded.

They collected themselves, turned to walk away, and stopped.

*****

In their path, stood a small boy. He was a little taller than Alfredo, but human indeed. Disheveled, dirty, wearing worn tan clothing and a small turban, threadbare and hanging down the right side of his face. He smiled, nodded, held his cupped hands forward. A beggar, no doubt.

They had no time for beggars. "I am sorry, boy," Fymurip said. "But we've no time for you."

"Will you look into my hands, fair lady?" The boy asked.

Reflexively, Catherine leaned forward and looked towards the boy's hands. Before she spoke, the boy opened his palms, and the snake struck.

Faster than Fymurip could respond, the small, copper-colored asp uncoiled and sunk its fangs into Catherine's throat. She gasped and fell backward. Fymurip caught her before she struck the ground. He laid her gently down and tore the snake away, crushing its head in his fist and casting it aside.

The small puncture wounds on her throat leaked blood and green poison. Catherine gasped for air and clutched at her throat. "What - what is happening - " she tried to speak.

"Shhh," Fymurip whispered to her. "Be still. Don't move."

He drew his dagger and put a small cut near the bite. Then he leaned in to suck the poison from her wound.

An ear-piercing shriek echoed through the street.

Fymurip spit poison, fell back, and looked into the sky.

It was dark, so the shape did not become clear until it was nearly upon them. At first, Fymurip thought it *Cuélebre*, but no. As it descended, its long, sharp beak and its massive, bird-like head transitioned into the body of a lion, with claws outstretched to shred anything in its path. It swooped down into the street with a rush of wind off its mighty wings. Those onlookers foolish enough to stand near toppled backwards as the wind off those wings cast them aside. Fymurip stood quickly, braced himself against the rush of wind, and drew his blades.

But the griffin did not let upon the ground. It flew down the street, like an arrow, its keen eyes fixed on Catherine, its claws open and forward. Fymurip stood his ground over his lady love and waited.

The impetus of the beast was too great. Like a petal on the wind, Fymurip was pushed aside. As he fell backwards, he managed to land a cut on the beast's right claw and had the satisfaction of hearing a screech of pain, before being thrown into a nearby wall.

The griffin shrieked again, opened its claw wider, and plucked Catherine off the ground. Before Fymurip could recover, she was gone.

IV

VI

He ran after them, a mile at least, until the shadow of the griffin against the strong moonlight disappeared and the beast's shrieks dissipated. He shouted her name so many times his throat hurt. His face was so wet with tears it felt like rain. She was gone, he had to accept, and what could he do about it? He had no idea where she was being taken. And who had taken her? Her father? The Inquisition? The Hanseatic League? Or someone else? In her line of work, there were a number of possibilities. And why the asp? Why poison her? Well, it was obvious once he took a moment to calm down and think about it: it kept her from fighting back, getting free in flight, and falling to her death as the griffin winged her off to wherever it was taking her. Fymurip just hoped he had sucked enough of the poison out of her body to keep it from working. Obviously, whoever had taken her wasn't too concerned about whether she lived or died at the end of the journey.

The boy with the snake was gone, of course, and to no surprise, no one was talking. They saw nothing. Heard nothing, even when Fymurip grew angry and smacked a few younger men for their lack of consideration at his questions. They came at him strong, but when he drew his sword and dagger, they backed down. All for the best, he knew, for if they had challenged him in the mood he was in, two sons would not be coming home tonight.

He had never felt so helpless in his life. Even in the pits, when he fought for his life, Fymurip always knew that the situation was, at least, fair. He had weapons, and his opponent had weapons. They faced off across a pit of sand and knew what the outcome could be. Here, his opponent (whoever that might be) had not given him a chance to fight back. And now, as he walked the dark Cairo streets looking for Alfredo, he worried that his one slash of his sword against the griffon had been too strong and that the creature would die in flight, crash into the sea, and Catherine with it. Oh, so many emotions rolling through his mind. Fymurip had felt a lot of pain in his life, but never pain like this.

An hour later, he found the Trasgo in the Maydan al Qahaq,

the main training ground for Mamluk cavalry, and despite the late hour, at least a full regiment was conducting maneuvers to torch and lamplight. The sounds of commanders barking orders, hoof beats against the hard Egyptian soil, and the fwang! of bowstrings releasing waves of arrows against padded targets was almost deafening.

Before Alfredo could react, Fymurip grabbed him up and pushed him against a stone post. It felt good to hear the little devil gasp for air as Fymurip's fingers dug into his thin neck. "She's gone, you son of a bitch. She's gone."

"Wh—who?" Alfredo asked as he tried to pry Fymurip's fingers away from his throat.

Fymurip told him everything, and it seemed in the telling that Alfredo genuinely did not know what had happened, nor was happy about it. As he laid out the story, he released the Trasgo and let him drop to the ground.

Alfredo regained his breath, wiggled his head, straightened out his vest and short drab white pantaloons, and said, "I apologize, sir. I did not anticipate an attack against fair Catherine. But I am sure she will be fine."

"How can you know? She was ripped away by a griffin."

"Yes, and do you know how difficult it is to summon such a creature? How expensive? Someone who would go to such trouble has no intention of allowing their prize to be harmed in any way. I assure you; she will be safe."

But she is not here. Fymurip wanted to say it aloud, as if doing so would somehow make her abduction go away, and the events of the past few days a bad dream. He pinched his eyes shut, but when he opened them, everything was the same. "I don't know if I can do this without her. I don't know."

"Of course, you can," Alfredo said, "and you must. She could not have helped you in this endeavor anyway. There can only be one warrior to face Cuélebre."

Fymurip shook his head. "I am no Rodrigo Díaz de Vivar, Alfredo. I am no El Cid."

"No, you are not, but you'll do. Now," Alfredo said, pushing against Fymurip's leg as if he were pushing a stone. "Go... go."

Fymurip allowed himself to be pushed. "And do what?"

"You said you were a cavalry soldier for Sultan Beyazid, correct? Then be one again. Go, and train."

*****

Through Alfredo's connections, Fymurip was given a horse, fresh clothing (which felt and looked more Turkish than Arabic), a bow, and a full quiver of arrows. Several quivers, in fact, for he would spend a few days training, as the little Trasgo had said. And by the end of the first day, Fymurip could barely move.

He took quickly to riding again. It felt like walking, as if being on horseback was an inherent ability given to him by Allah. What was less easy to recall was bow work. Fymurip understood the basics of using a compound bow, of course, understood how to aim and release, but he had spent the last few years working his sword and dagger, together exclusively, like they were mere extensions of his arms. One could easily see the bow in similar fashion, he supposed, but the mechanics were different, and required a steady aim, a keen eye. When the horse was still, Fymurip could hit the target easily enough. When it was in motion, his aim was less impressive. His legs hurt, his back hurt. Everything hurt. And his trainer would not allow him to finish his first day until he was able to strike the target effectively at a trot. The Mamluks prided themselves in their mounted archery; their armies lived and died by the effectiveness of their light cavalry.

On day two, he spent the morning conducting Furusiyah, a system of physical and military training that Mamluk amirs required of their soldiers. The training was shortened to a few simple, yet important, duties, such as cavalry soldiers having to put on and take off their armor while riding. Footmen were required to use their swords, shields, and spears in various ways, in various formations, and be able to change formations quickly to address changing dangers on the battlefield. In the afternoon, a regiment of freeborn halq footmen were added to the training for coordinated maneuver with the cavalry. Fymurip was impressed at the preparation. It was clear that Sultan al Ghuri was serious about meeting the Turks on the battlefield. But their numbers were small… so, so small. The Mamluk army was certainly larger than he could count, but by Fymurip's estimation, it was no more than twenty thousand men, and that included support troopers and the supply carts and camels (more camels than Fymurip had ever seen). There was hope that they would pick up more soldiers as they marched through the Levant and into Syria. There were Turkomens and Kurds and Anatolians there loyal to al

Ghuri. Perhaps their addition would swell the ranks another ten or fifteen thousand. But that would not be enough to defeat the Ottomans.

What of the dragon? Was its power equivalent to a regiment? More? Fymurip could not say, for he had never seen it in battle. It would be powerful, no doubt about that, but the Turks also had their fair share of supernatural weapons.

Cuélebre's shrieks echoed across the Cairo night, and the long line of sheep and goats that Fymurip could see in the distance, being herded together to make the long march, made Fymurip wonder if the dragon's presence was too costly. Just how much food did a dragon require to keep it satisfied? Once in battle, it could eat whatever it killed, but getting there, and keeping it under control... Was it worth the cost? He guessed they would all find out soon enough. On the morning of the fourth day, Fymurip and the Mamluk army marched to war.

VI

Into the Levant they marched, for days, passing the towns of Gaza, Ramleh, Jaffa, and all along being greeted as conquerors, liberators, saviors, for it was clear to Fymurip that this part of the Mamluk Empire truly feared the Ottomans, and with good reason. Their military numbers were enthusiastic and willing, but again, small. Without al-Ghuri and his army - and now, his dragon - the Turks could easily sweep up these outlying communities and bend them to their will. Each town they passed added soldiers to al Ghuri's ranks, and by the time they reached the outskirts of Damascus, the army was near thirty thousand. Still too small a number for Fymurip's taste, but better, and with the dragon... well, perhaps they'd have a chance. A slim one, indeed, but a chance, nonetheless.

They marched in column, with cavalry in the van- and rear-guard, to screen the infantry and the dragon. The beast itself was controlled by three dozen Eldar priests and, by Fymurip's estimation, a ton of chains, ropes, cords, and anything else that could be strapped around its ample girth. Somehow, they had managed to wrap chains around its snout, thus keeping it from roaring and spouting fire. That was good, for too many outbursts of that nature and al Ghuri's dreams of a Turkish defeat would wither. Fymurip made a point to keep his distance from the dragon. Despite the fact that al Ghuri and his guard were no longer interested in Fymurip now that they had El Cid's dragon, it would not do to linger near the beast for fear of a reconsideration of that policy. Also, if Fymurip were honest with himself, he was afraid of it. Who wouldn't be? It seemed to have grown since its release from Tizona and Colada, and it didn't look like it had any interest in stopping that growth. He kept his distance, until such time as he needed to draw near... per Alfredo's plan.

There were many times on the march that Fymurip wanted to speak to Alfredo about the plan, to gain clarification on certain bits of it, but the little Trasgo marched with al Ghuri himself, with duties that took him very close to Cuélebre.

As they drew closer to Damascus, some of the citizens weren't as helpful, and oftentimes, threatening. Their closeness to Turkish influence was obvious to Fymurip, and so their allegiance to the Mamluks was suspect at best. These people had the most difficult life, not knowing which power to welcome, which to rebuke. But once they saw the dragon, however, being hauled in chains to the battlefield, their truculence subsided and their declaration for al Ghuri grew forceful.

Fymurip and his squadron of cavalry raided communities that resisted al Ghuri's call for aide, even after seeing Cuélebre. Their orders were to take, by force, any and all provisions denied the Sultan, and then compel, by sword and spear, all able-bodied men and boys to take up arms with the Mamluks in protection of their kingdom. Those who refused could be executed. Fymurip, as diplomatically as possible, always seemed to be somewhere else in the raiding party when executions were doled out. He was not about to participate in such a brutal act. It wasn't as if such harsh measures weren't taken by the Ottomans when necessary; all armies seemed to revel in terrorizing their citizenry. Fymurip knew that it was a failing in the human spirit and a weakness in all leaders that drove them to order such punishment. It was a sign of the times, a sign of things to come. Fymurip kept his head down and did his duty.

On one such raid, he found a wooden box of vials that its owner tried to bury right before the Mamluks arrived. Fymurip recognized the vials immediately.

"Do you know what these are?" Fymurip asked as he held up one of the vials of red-hot liquid. He faced his commander. "Do you know what they can do?"

"Of course, I know what they are," his amir said, though from the tall man's expression, it was clear that he did not. "Do you take me for a fool?"

Yes, Fymurip thought, but said instead, "I have seen this action before. The Ottomans have pre-positioned these throughout their client states, and as our armies pass, they will release them in our rear to bite and snap and harass our approach, and we will be pulled in two different directions, and destroyed piecemeal."

His commander snatched the vial from Fymurip's hand and gazed into the red liquid. "Nonsense. There is hardly a drop of liquid in there. It's harmless. I'll show you."

"No, don't..."

But before Fymurip could stop him, the foolish amir uncorked the vial, and out rushed a small efreet, no larger than a dog.

It whirled itself into a funnel of fire, engulfed the tent that they were standing in, and burned the amir alive. Fymurip barely made it out of the conflagration before the other vials popped open from the heat and added their rage to the growing funnel. Before the efreets dissipated in the dry air of the evening, the amir and his command staff were dead, and a third of the regiment was cooked beyond recognition.

The next morning, Fymurip was given command of what was left of the regiment. He accepted the position humbly, with a congratulatory visit from Alfredo.

"The plan is coming together nicely," the little beast said, then left quickly.

Three days later, on a flat, clean battlefield just south of Tripoli, the two armies gathered.

In the early darkness of the next morning, Sultan al Ghuri sent his lieutenants their order: When the rising sun is upon your back... attack!

*****

The Mamluk army arrayed itself for battle with its impressive infantry contingent on the left and its cavalry on the right. This was the traditional disposition of troops and had carried them from victory to victory in the past, even against smaller Turkish armies. But the army arrayed against them across the empty, deadly stretch of rugged land in between, was no normal army. It was massive, and from where Fymurip waited - atop a small ridgeline that commanded the field and blocked view of the dragon, Sultan Bayezid's Ottoman army was a wonder to behold.

It was arrayed with infantry in the middle, and cavalry on both flanks. Akinji light cavalry had been pushed out a few hundred feet ahead of the main body, to screen and to receive the initial charge of the Mamluks. Azab infantry waited in tight blocks behind, interspersed with small units of Janissary hand gunners to protect their flanks. The main body of Janissary was further behind the front lines, held in reserve for that critical moment where their skill and quality would be needed. Pushed in between the lighter infantry and cavalry were the heavier Spahi cavalry, some of the Porte and some feudal. Fymurip could also spot a few banners of Dellis cavalry, and even some of his own Tatar provincials. And on its own ridgeline, behind the army itself, was a line of Turkish cannon, their barrels glistening in the rising sun, their crews quiet, still, and ready to drive screaming balls of iron and Allah knew what else, into oncoming Mamluk chargers.

The Turks were ready.

So too were the Mamluks, or so it seemed to Fymurip. No sign of fear or unease could he see on anyone's faces, especially his own men, whom he knew had doubts about his ability to lead them into the fray. Fymurip had doubts about that as well, but that really wasn't the plan that he had agreed to with Alfredo. Yes, he was to lead his cavalry into the battle, but then... Well, he'd see what happened after that.

Amirs called to their men, riding their horses up and down the Mamluk line, rousing them to courage and great deeds, shoring up any fears they might have, any doubts. Their men responded in kind, repeating the words back to their commanders, banging their spears on their shields, stamping their boots, their sandals, throwing bolts from their crossbows into the air towards the enemy. Fymurip did the same with his men, lifting his bow into the air as he straddled his horse and cried for Ottoman blood in his best Arabic. He even felt a chill race down his spine at the martial intensity of it all. Indeed, it felt good to be among warriors again: Elite Khassakis holding the center of the infantry line; Halqa infantrymen guarding their flanks; Rammaha lancers; Ashir Syrian Auxiliaries; and archers and crossbowmen, as far as the eye could see. A veritable sea of men with shields and spears and bows and lances, covered head to toe in leather, lamellar, and chainmail armor. Banners waving in the air. Drums sounding out tempo at every shout and war cry echoing across the arid field. It was all wondrous, exciting, and Fymurip nearly lost himself in its awesome pageantry.

Then the dragon roared, and not a muffled roar that he had heard for days on the march. The chains around its snout had been removed for sure, and it bellowed its rage, its discomfort, for all to hear.

Both armies seemed shocked at the roar, but the Turks more so than the Mamluks, whose horses, thankfully, had been partially trained within eyeshot of the terrible beast. Collectively, it seemed as if the Turks fell back a few desperate paces, and Fymurip could see some waver in the infantry ranks. But Bayezid's lieutenants took charge of their men's apprehension quickly and brought the matter to a close.

Then, far in the distance, three lone Akinji horsemen rode out from their screening line, side by side, quiet and unassuming. Fymu-rip squinted through the rising sun and heat of the day and watched as these Turkish soldiers stopped about one hundred feet from their army, pulled their horses up together, and then drew arrows. They notched them in composite bows, drew their arms back, aimed into the sky, and let loose.

Three thin, harmless arrows flew into the morning sky. Then they burst into flames, and from their narrow bodies snaked three fire serpents, growing larger and larger, until they were each twenty to twenty-five feet in length. They roiled and coiled their way up into the sky, like braided rope, and then they descended, like fire rain, towards the Mamluk infantry line.

Before they struck, a half dozen Khassakis emerged from their infantry blocks, scooped up handfuls of pebbles, dirt, and sand, and flung it into the air towards the falling fire snakes. The dirt and sand formed a choking cloud of dust that spread quickly and whirled into a foggy conflagration almost as strong and ominous as the fire snakes. From its center grew a face, then a head, and then thick black teeth that shot up out of the dirty cloud of dust and struck the fire snakes with great force.

The impact caused an explosion, and bits of fire and scorched rock and dirt showered both armies.

There was a pause, a long, agonizing pause. Both armies looked at each other across the field.

Then all hell broke loose.

VII

The lines charged. More fire creatures and dust devils were flung at each other. Some found purchase and burned or choked men as they ran towards one another with shields and swords and spears raised and ready. Other devilish, ethereal creatures were released on both sides. It seemed as if these armies were content with using minimal supernatural weapons, only the smaller, more manageable creatures designed for agitation and complication than for inflicting serious damage. But perhaps that would come later in the day, when both sides were spent and wavering. Perhaps...

Fymurip ordered his men off the ridgeline and into the fray with the rest of the charging Mamluk cavalry. Nearly five thousand strong, twenty thousand hooves beating the ground on a mile-wide advance that clearly outnumbered the Turks on the right flank. It was an impressive charge, with drums beating and red-and-yellow banners waving. There were so many horses that it seemed for a time that they would topple over one another, as Ottoman archers let loose a hornet's nest of arrows that blocked the light of the sun. But the Mamluks responded in kind, answering the rush of enemy arrows with a sea of their own, and the Mamluks were just superior archers from horseback. They rose up on their saddles, aimed carefully, despite the threat from incoming missiles, took aim, and brought down wave after wave of Turkish cavalry that fell forward and littered the ground with thousands of pounds of dead horse flesh.

Casualties began to mount on both sides, and the way forward became difficult. Some units stopped their advance, dismounted, and moved forward on foot. Mamluk crossbowmen did so in unison, forming lines and moving together, and when possible, using downed horses as shields against the incessant wave of Ottoman arrows.

Fymurip's regiment found a path around the growing piles of dead and charged with Rammaha lancers, straight into the flank of the Akinji light cavalry. Fymurip grew disgusted with his bow and threw it away, drew his sword and dagger, and tore into the terrified Turks. Two, three, four cavalrymen were taken down quickly, before they could draw their own weapons in response. He felt good, better than he had in a long while, and he relished in the fight, despite knowing that at any moment, a stray arrow, an errant bolt, a lucky spear, could pierce his heart and end it all right there. Then so be it, he thought as he hacked and slashed and stabbed his way through Turk after Turk. If I die now, then my struggle is over. I will have peace. But he didn't really mean it. Not yet, anyway. There were still things he needed to do on this terrible day of death and desolation. Things that needed to be done before he could die.

Fymurip could not see how the rest of the fight was going. He could only see a few feet in front of him, but he could hear the roar of the infantry in the distance, the clamber of metal on metal, the barked orders from anxious amirs, the ear-piercing screams of death. The world entire seemed at war, and he an important part of it. A small part, indeed, only one man on a field of tens of thousands. But at this moment, nothing in all the world mattered but the blades in his hand, the horse between his legs, and the enemy soldiers he faced.

Cannon fire erupted on the hill behind the Ottoman line. Massive balls of iron ripped through the right flank, hitting both Turks and Mamluks, but their impetus took them straight through line after line of Mamluk cavalry. Whole bodies were shattered, heads exploded, limbs tossed into the air. The cannon balls that flew through Fymurip's ranks seemed to be intelligent, seemed to know exactly where to strike, and then he saw why. Each ball had a small jinn attached to it, some blue, some white, but all with wings as they tipped left or right as needed to direct the balls into the juiciest, most deadly, positions on the Mamluk line. Fymurip dropped from his saddle just as his horse was ripped in two by a whistling ball. He rolled out of harm's way and came to rest against the body of a mangled horse.

"Release the dragon! Release the dragon!" Fymurip screamed the words out loud, over and over, as if the men controlling the beast could hear. But what other choice did the Mamluks have? If it wasn't released soon, al-Ghuri's army would be routed. He did not know how the rest of the battle was faring, but here, on the place where he cowered behind dead horses, to shield himself from jinn-controlled cannon fire, it was just a matter of time before Mamluk cavalry began to rout.

And then it appeared, out from behind the ridgeline. It flapped its long, leathery wings and rose up into the morning sunlight, providing shade as it flew. It roared, and a gout of fire burst from its toothy mouth and scorched the ground for a hundred feet as it dipped its serpentine head to survey the battlefield. Both sides of the fight seemed to pause as *Cuélebre* flew across the main battle line. Turkish arrows tracked its flight, and a thousand shafts struck its thick hide. Some stuck in its flesh, but most bounced off harmlessly. *Cuélebre* answered with more fire, and Turkish bowmen burned.

The cannons turned and opened fire on the dragon. Their jinn companions were able to guide the balls directly into *Cuélebre's* path, and some exploded against its chest and rocked it backwards. For a moment, a cheer went up among the Turks as *Cuélebre* wavered in the air. But their joy was short-lived, as the dragon righted itself and redirected its attack on the hill where the cannon were positioned. It dodged another volley of cannonballs, flew up higher, realigned itself with the ridgeline, drew back its long neck as if it were drawing a lungful of air, and then it released more flames.
The ridgeline, and the Ottoman cannon, burned.

*****

A thick, black smoke came off the wooden cannon mounts. The barrels themselves melted like lava, and without their cannon, the Ottomans shook. Some infantry regiments in the center broke, and it seemed for a short time that the Mamluks would command the field.

Then the janissaries, being held in reserve, began to move forward. Fymurip could not tell how many there were. A thousand perhaps, maybe more. But they were almost an army unto themselves, and they stood like stone against a wave of lesser men who routed past them and straight into *Cuélebre's* fire. These once Christian men stood as the jewel of the Ottoman force, and they held their position well. While the rest of the army tried desperately to salvage a victory, while it tried to control the dragon that was spitting fire into the retreating Ottoman lines, they took the center of the field and anchored it. Suddenly, those who were retreating stopped, re-formed their lines alongside the janissaries, and moved back into the fight.

Fymurip's embattled cavalry was beginning to waver. He could not tell how many men he had lost, but the numbers were high. Only with the dragon destroying the cannon did they suddenly feel emboldened and continued to fight, using both men and horse as redoubt against dismounted Ottomans who seemed more skilled with the sword then their Mamluk counterparts. Disgusted, Fymurip spit into the ground and wished that he too could breathe fire. It would certainly make things easier for him at this moment, watching his men die all around, doing as much as he could to try to stop it, and yet doing so little. In truth, he didn't know what to do. He could not order a general retreat; he wasn't sure that he had the authority to do so, and even if he did, would it be followed?

He had another problem as well. He needed to get to Alfredo who was somewhere near the center of the Mamluk line, somewhere near al-Ghuri and his personal guard. That was the plan. That had always been the plan. But plans never go as expected when armies meet on the field, and how could he steal a horse and abandon his men?

The janissaries made his decision much easier.

Having moved forward and thus stopped the Ottoman retreat, they now formed into attack lines, spear- and swordsmen in the center, hand gunners on the flanks. They moved forward, pushing the uncertain, confused Mamluk infantry back, back, until they were standing close to their original positions. Fymurip watched as best he could from the killing ground around him, occasionally taking a spear thrust or sword swing and handing it back to his assailant in spades. The entire right flank was a mangle of dismounted men and those still capable of riding. It was hard to know who was who, as the bodies piled up and the ground grew saturated with blood. Fymurip's arms ached like they had never ached before as he tried staying strong and keeping his eyes on the janissary advance.

Cuélebre now turned its attention to the janissaries, but they were ready. It was difficult to know for sure, but Fymurip could swear that as they passed Mamluk dead, men within the janissary ranks knelt down and pushed their hands into the blood of those dead, coming up with red hands, and then holding those hands up to the sky, and then chanting in unison some form of spell. Fymurip's heart sank, for he knew what they were doing, had seen it done once before in the Ottoman army in which he had been a member. There was no chance now to ignore his agreement with Alfredo, and he had to act now, before any more Mamluk corpses were deprived of blood.

"You are in charge now," Fymurip shouted at a young boy nearby. "You are in charge. Take charge... order your men to re-form and attack!"

Before the terrified young man could respond, Fymurip was up and running towards the infantry line, towards the center, where he believed Alfredo and al-Ghuri still remained.

He wound his way through halqa troopers, both cavalry and infantry. He dodged and weaved his way through confused, bloody lines of battle. He tried keeping his head down and moving forward, but he could not stop himself from pausing when able to see what was happening with Cuélebre and the janissaries.

At least a dozen of them had bloody hands raised to the sky while hand gunners on both flanks took aim at the dragon and tried keeping it from killing them all with fire. Handguns were not very accurate, and they required en masse firing to be effective. They fired together and showered the dragon's face, mouth, and neck with bullets to keep it from rearing back and spitting. It held the beast at bay just long enough for those with bloody hands to do their work.

Blood magic. Fymurip had seen it before. Traditionally, efreets — the biggest and most powerful - were born from the unsettled blood of an enemy, and what began to swirl out of the collective raised hands of those men were even larger than the efreet, Ufaj, Fymurip had met in Istanbul. And there were more than just one. Each man with bloody hands created his own, a dozen at least. From their hands shot hot, flaming efreets, every bit as deadly and ominous as *Cuélebre*, who now noticed the deadly jinns rising from the janissary ranks. The dragon grew angry, desperate, and it blew a powerful gout of fire straight into the rising efreets, but that only seemed to make them stronger.

The efreets rose up, collected themselves, and then attacked the dragon.

Now, even the janissaries fell back as a battle raged above them. Nothing but fire could Fymurip see as he tried reaching the center of the battlefield. The efreets swarmed the dragon like ants and tried choking it from snout to tail, like a constrictor snake. But the spikes along the dragon's body make it difficult for them to gain purchase. The flames that they created were so bright that it felt to Fymurip as if the sun had fallen from the sky, and the heat that they gave off was unbearable.

But he pressed forward. As the efreets slammed the dragon to the ground and crawled over it with relentless fury, he found al-Ghuri's headquarters, and he found Alfredo... with a spear sticking out of his back.

VIII

VIII

Fymurip rolled the Trasgo over and held him in his arms. The head of the spear had pierced straight through his chest, but he was alive.

"Where is the Sultan?" Fymurip asked.

Alfredo coughed up phlegm and blood. Fymurip gnashed his teeth, but respectfully wiped drool from the goblin's mouth. Alfredo coughed again.

"He's retreated, even in the face of victory. Like a coward."

"Well, it looks like the janissaries will have the dragon soon enough," Fymurip said, looking around to make sure they were in a safe position. Scores of the Sultan's personal guard lay in bloody heaps all around. "You can be at peace now."

Alfredo shook his head, coughed. "No. That will not stop it. You must do what we have discussed. Soon, it will rise again, and you must kill it. You must kill it, or all of Europe will burn. Catherine will burn."

"I can't—I—"

"You must! Now go. Go as we have discussed and do little-Alfredo one last kindness."

The trago's eyes rolled back, his head went limp, and he died. Fymurip whispered a small prayer, laid the creature down, and stood.

Everywhere, battle still raged, and it was difficult to know who had the advantage. Where one flank wavered, the other reformed. Even in the center where, despite the ball of fire that roiled back and forth as the efreets and the dragon fought, the janissaries met the last complete and unbroken block of Khassaki infantry. The horror and bloodshed that raged there was enough to upend any man's stomach, and Fymurip tried his best not to be distracted from his duty.

And what was that duty? To kill the dragon, of course, as he and Alfredo had discussed. But what a stupid idea; an idea that grew more and more foolish with each passing moment, as Fymurip stood and watched Cuélebre devour one efreet after another, as Alfredo had implied it would. But of course, it would do that; Fymurip felt silly not realizing that would happen. Efreets, despite their power, were finite, and had to attack quickly and decisively to be effective. That's why the janissaries had flung a dozen against the dragon. But they could have flung a thousand and it would have done no good. Fymurip realized that now. For the dragon was infinite, so long as its weakness was not known by its enemy. And no one knew Cuéle-bre's weakness, except Alfredo. And now, Fymurip.

One after another, the efreets were torn apart and devoured by the dragon, until there were none left. The dragon gulped down the final efreet, and then belched it back up with a line of fire that cut through the janissary line.

Sultan Beyazid's finest then routed.

But *Cuélebre* did not pursue. It had been victorious. It was alive, indeed. But it was spent, tired, exhausted, in fact, as it sat there on the ground like a lump of rock, unmoving, trying to regain its strength. A few bold janissaries tried to attack it with spears, tried puncturing its softer underbelly. But that wasn't its weakness, and it simply smacked the men aside with its head.

Fymurip breathed deeply, closed his eyes, and prayed one last time to Allah. Oh, how he longed for a mosque, to kneel prop-erly, to pray with fellow Muslims. He had been too long away from such activity. It felt good to think about it, and he hoped someday he'd be able to do so, in Mecca. What a wonderful feeling that would be.

He opened his eyes and drew his sword, his dagger. He walked out into the battlefield, towards the dragon.

His heart raced. He felt like passing out. He paused several times, but always did he move forward, towards *Cuélebre*, until there was nothing but a few feet between him and the dragon's snout. The dragon seemed nonplussed by Fymurip's approach. What could one man possibly do to him, anyway? The glimmer in the dragon's eyes, eyes almost as large as Fymurip himself, was one of amusement, curiosity. This lone, small, insignificant little man, approaching the mighty *Cuélebre*. The dragon seemed to almost smile at the nerve of it, and it watched quietly as Fymurip approached.

Fymurip breathed deeply and held up his blades. His entire body shook in fear, but he held his weapons aloft and said in the most powerful voice that he could muster, "O Mighty *Cuélebre*, hear me, for I am Rodrigo Díaz de Vivar.

"I am El Cid."

*****

The dragon's mouth did not move, but Fymurip could hear the serpent's voice in his mind.

El Cid? That name is familiar to me.

"It should be familiar," Fymurip said aloud. "I am that man."

Cuélebre's mighty eyes blinked as it moved its head closer to get a better view. Fymurip stood his ground, though he could feel his bowel loosen. He tightened his stance, gripped his sword and dagger, and blinked back.

The El Cid that I remember was a taller man, stronger. He had a beard and a full suit of armor. You have none of those things. His skin was lighter too. He was a mighty warrior, and I was proud to die at his hand, to then occupy his swords, so that I might one day rise again. You are not *El Campeador*. He was a giant.

"I am that man… and I have come to kill you again."

The dragon laughed, in his mind. To Fymurip, if felt like a tickle, but he did not share the dragon's mirth. He could barely hold himself upright in the midst of the sickly-sweet sulfur smell that emanated from Cuélebre's mouth, like fog from a steaming glade. No man…no one, can kill me. Go away, silly little creature, and let me alone. I am risen. I have empires to destroy, and gold to steal.

The dragon turned to walk away, and Fymurip pounced.

He took his dagger and thrust it forward into Cuélebre's eye. It was a soft spot on the dragon, indeed, but not its true vulnerability. That did not matter, however, as the blow was to just prick the creature, to agitate its eye, make it bleed a little, to weaken its eyesight. That was the first step of the plan.

The dragon roared and spit flames towards Fymurip. The Tatar jumped out of the way in time, feeling only the sear of fire against his clothing. He rolled, came back up, jumped towards the dragon inside the swing of its tail, and attacked again, this time driving his dagger underneath a scale and slicing through tender flesh.

Cuélebre roared again, angry for certain that it had been caught off-guard twice. These minor attacks by such small blades were nothing, but Fymurip could see that the beast's pride was beginning to turn foul. "You cannot seem to stop me, O might Cuélebre," Fymurip said as he danced past a swipe from the dragon's razor-sharp claws. "Maybe you are not as powerful as you claim, your legendary eyesight not so good."

Foolish man! If an army cannot destroy me, how can you?

"I told you. I am Rodrigo Diaz de Vivar. I am El Cid. I am *El Campeador*. I defeated you once before. I will do so again."

Around and around the large belly of the dragon, Fymurip poked and slashed and did very little in way of damage. But *Cuélebre* twisted and turned as if he were trying to catch a fly or mosquito that kept jumping just out of reach. Around and around like a dog chasing its tail. Fymurip too was growing weary of the second part of Alfredo's plan to agitate and anger. He could not keep it up much longer. His legs were weakening, his arms were heavy, and his lungs gasped for air. But not yet, not quite yet. It was almost time, but he needed a little more time, just a little more.

Fymurip slashed the dragon's neck and then ran straight away, towards a large clump of hand-sized rocks near the Mamluk battle line. The armies now had dispersed from this part of the battlefield, neither one wishing to get involved in his dance with the serpent. Fymurip moved in a jagged line, back and forth, left and right, not giving the dragon a clear shot at him as he moved. Cuélebre tried, spitting out line after line of fire to catch Fymurip, but all he did was scorch and bake the ground around Fymurip's feet, broiling the rocks until they glowed hot red.

Perfect, Fymurip thought, as he did a few circles around the rock bed until they were all red hot and simmering. Just as Alfredo predicted.

Then a line of the dragon's breath caught Fymurip in the leg. He screamed. This was not part of the plan, but what could he do? He fell, amidst the hot bed of rocks, trying desperately not to burn himself to death among them. His leg ached as he dropped his dagger and patted out the fire that peeled away the skin on his right calf. The pain was excruciating, and Fymurip almost passed out. What saved him from doing so was the dragon itself.

Cuélebre roared in satisfaction, raised himself onto his hind legs, and then launched. It was more of a hop than a flight. The dragon rose upon its large wings, and then immediately set back down near the steaming bed of rocks.

Fymurip crawled backward, pushing the rocks out of his way as he crawled. The pain in his leg, however, was gone, now that he was again faced with Cuélebre's mighty eye.

You thought you could kill me? The dragon chucked into a roar. Humans will never learn. I am immortal. I am infinite. I—

But humans do learn, if they are wise enough to listen. And that's what Fymurip had done: despite his anger and distrust of the little creature, he had listened to Alfredo's plan, for he and the dragon were both Asturian, both borne from the same supernatural powers that had first birthed them into the world. First step blind the eye so that *Cuélebre* could not see well; second step, agitate, agitate, agitate, until the beast was so enraged that it ignored any dangers; third step, find a red-hot stone. For a red-hot, burning stone would bring it down, so the legend told. And how perfect was it that they were fighting in the Levant, a place where the ground was littered with rocks. El Cid had not defeated *Cuélebre* in combat; that was the public lie that the world had accepted. Even the dragon, in its centuries of time to reflect on its demise trapped in El Cid's swords, had come to believe it. No. El Cid had listened to the stories and fables of his country and had learned from past mistakes.

Now Fymurip reached for one of those rocks. He gripped the biggest he could find. He screamed as its heat burned his hand. But he did not let go, and as Cuélebre reared up to deliver a final spray of fire, Fymurip tossed the rock into the dragon's mouth.

Cuélebre swallowed as if it were eating, shocked by the sudden appearance of something in its throat. It fell back, gasped for air, which came as tiny drools of fire down its dark, horned chin. It tried clearing its throat, but the rock must have slipped further down its throat, for Fymurip could clearly see the coloring of the dragon's scales grow dark red.

The dragon fell back, twisted and turned and slammed its head and neck against the ground, trying desperately to dislodge the stone. It could not breathe. It could not spit fire. It could not talk, for Fymurip heard no words in his mind, nothing save for the wet, terrified sounds of a creature dying.

He did not pause. Alfredo said that once the stone was in place, Fymurip must strike, strike! And hard. And so he did. He crawled to his discarded dagger, took it in his burnt hand. He held his sword tightly in the other, rose up on weak legs. The pain from his burning calf leeched up his thigh. He could barely stand. But he endured, and walked, slowly, slowly, towards *Cuélebre* until again, he faced the creature's eye. A wounded eye.

"I am sorry, *Cuélebre*," Fymurip said, raising his dagger and sword above his head. "I truly am. Perhaps you do not deserve to die in this manner, and perhaps you will have another day. But not this day. Today, I vanquish you in the name of Catherine, a bright daughter of Spain. Long may she live."

Then Fymurip screamed and drove his sword and dagger deep into the dragon's eye.

It took a little while for such a mighty creature to die. Fymurip turned his blades again and again, until they were thrust deep into Cuélebre's brain. He was shoulder deep in eye juice, blood, bile. What a sickening scene it was! But he kept turning and thrusting those blades until the dragon stopped shaking, belched a tiny sliver of fire, then died.

*****

He must have passed out, for when Fymurip awoke, it was twilight, and a cool breeze blew across the battlefield.

The dragon lay at his side, its head shielding Fymurip from the last stands of light from the setting sun. It eye was a gaping hole, and Fymurip's sword and dagger lay beneath it, covered in ooze and gore.

Where were the armies? He did not know. Who won? That was even less apparent, as both Mamluk and Ottoman bodies lay everywhere.

Fymurip sat up, stretched his back, looked around. He was in pain. His leg still hurt, but not as much as before. And the dragon was dead. *Cuélebre* was dead. That, more than anything, mattered.

Slowly, he stood, stretched again, then picked up his blades. He wiped them clean on the dragon's scales. He took a moment to look around further, trying to see if anyone was left, anyone near that he could walk to, to talk to, to learn what had happened.

He was alone.

But for the dragon, and praise Allah, it was dead. Fymurip almost smiled. He'd done it. He had followed the plan, and it had worked, despite Catherine's misgivings. He could hardly believe it. *Cuélebre* was dead indeed, and the world was a safer place because of it.

He took one last look at the dragon. In its own way, it was beautiful, even in death. Still and stone-like, but the light from the setting sun made its tough hide and scales sparkle like water in a clear lake. Fymurip nodded to it and raised his sword in appreciation for such a powerful and valiant adversary.

He walked across the bloody field and through the bed of rocks that not long ago were as hot as lava. Now they were cool, though they steamed and smelled awful. He thanked them, chuckled at that, and longed for water. He took another step, and lightning flashed behind him.

Fymurip turned, and the last thing he saw before a portal opened and sucked him into a dark void, was Catherine's face.

How long he was in that darkness, he did not know. It seemed to stretch out forever. It was like floating on water, and in his mind, he tried to drink. But it was not water. Just darkness, emptiness. I am dying, he thought as he turned over and over like a leaf in the breeze. I am dying.

Then there was light, almost as powerful as the light from *Cuélebre's* fire. Light and then he struck ground.

Not the ground of the Levant, hard, dry, and rocky. This was grass, wet and cool. He gnashed his teeth against the pain of striking the ground so hard, but nothing had broken.

Fymurip blinked thrice, wiped his face clean, and pushed himself up on weak elbows. He arched his back and stared into the face of a knight.

"Good to see you again, old friend," Lux von Junker said and smiled. "What took you so long?"

EPILOGUE

The arrow struck the griffin square in the breast, right above the heart. The griffin itself was the most shocked, as nothing - no mortal weapon at least - could ever have harmed it. But the tip of the shaft barreled through its tough skin and thick feathers, striking true. It screeched, flapped its wings, tried staying aloft, but there was something more on the arrow tip than a sharp edge, and thus, it lost consciousness and fell.

Down and down it dropped, like a burning rock from heaven, straight towards the waters of the Mediterranean.

Catherine of Aragon, whom the beast had clutched in its strong talons, opened her eyes and fought against the poison coursing through her own body. She barely realized what had happened when they struck the water.

At first, she sunk like that stone from heaven, with the weight of the griffin pushing her down deep. But the first rush of saltwater in her lungs brought her to life again. She gagged, gulped water, opened her eyes, and began to wave her arms frantically, until she found her strength to reach the top.

I'm going to die here, she thought, cresting the waves and going down again. She was not a good swimmer. I'm going to die. But it might be best to die here, alone, in the middle of a sea, then at the hands of the man she considered her true father, for without doubt it had been Georg Cromer who had ordered her taken in Cairo. She had failed the League, she knew, and they had come after her. So, yes, best to die here, to drown alone, then to endure torture and belittlement at the hands of men she once respected.

She tried to die, but hands were on her quickly. One set, then two, as she was hoisted out of the water and onto a small boat. Then lips were on hers, but they were not the crude, forceful lips of a man. These were soft, smooth, and it almost felt as if she knew them, had felt them before, on her neck, her cheek. The mouth covering hers breathed life into her lungs. Three, four, five hard breaths.

Her eyes sprang open, and Catherine leaned over and blew seawater out of her lungs. Then she breathed, and God did it feel good. She gulped air as if she had never breathed a day in her life.

"That didn't take long."

The voice was very familiar. Catherine collected herself, pulled herself up, cleared her eyes, and stared into a face she had known all her life.

"Joanna?"

Juana la Loca smiled. "Good. You recognize your own sister. I was worried that the poison might have affected your mind."

Catherine coughed, cleared her throat. "But how... what... what is going on?"

"You have a lot of questions. I understand. But do you think I'd be content with staying in Zaragoza while father paced and complained and threatened to start wars to get you back? No, my sweet sister. Spain is not our concern right now; we shall leave it in the less-than-capable hands of our parents. You and I have a much more important mission to conduct."

"What mission?"

Joanna ignored the question, turned, and pointed at a carrack which sat anchored nearby. "Isn't she lovely? She's called the Santa Dominica, and the Order of Saint John has graciously given it to us for our journey."

Things were moving too fast. A moment ago, she was in the clutches of a griffin. Now, she was Joanna's guest on a mission to... where?

So much confusion roiled about in her mind. But the only thing that Catherine was able to say, was, "Where are we going?"

"To Albania, my sweet sister, and then, to Cathay, where a Teutonic Knight needs our help."

THE END

Bestiary

Cuélebre - A giant winged serpent of Asturian and Cantabrian mythology.

Lobisome - A Spanish werewolf, often used to guard castles and prisoners.

Trasgo Goblin - A domestic goblin of Asturian and Cantabrian mythology. Can often be found serving a particular person or persons its entire life, though, given its nature, can be mischievous and often dangerous.

Guisando Bulls - A set of Celtiberian sculptures located on the hill of Guisando in the municipality of El Tiemblo, Avila, Spain. It's believed that they were made during the 2nd century BCE. Though their physical nature is hard granite, each statue possesses a wandering spirit of a bull, and these spirits are often used by the Spanish Inquisition and other power bases (like the Crown) to warn and/or frighten undesirables out of Spain.

Griffin - A mythological creature with the body, tail, and back legs of a lion, and the head and wings of an eagle. These powerful and terrifying creatures are often used as supernatural agents by many organizations, including the Hanseatic League, to aide in their fight against the Eldar Gods.

Cherub Swarms - Servants of the Christian god, Cherubs are small child-like flying creatures whose original duty was to protect the Garden of Eden. But the centuries since then have changed and warped their purpose, and currently, they serve The Spanish Inquisition in swarms as trackers of heretics, Jews, and anyone (anything) else that their master, Diego de Deza, deems a threat to Spain and the Holy Catholic Church. They have tiny sharp teeth and their bite is intoxicating, often placing their victims in a stupor that takes days from which to fully recover.

Dramatis Personae

Diego de Deza - A theologian and the current Grand Inquisitor of Spain, having succeeded the dread Tomas de Torquemada. De Deza serves the Spanish crown unapologetically, and his mission is to rid Spain of all heretics, Jews, and servants of The Eldar Gods, or any other gods that do not comport with Christian dogma.

Queen Isabella I of Castile -The wife of Ferdinand II of Aragon and the mother of Catherine and Joanna (see below). She comes to power in 1479 and proves to be a formidable leader alongside her husband.

King Ferdinand II of Aragon - Often called The Catholic, he is the reigning King of Spain and the father of Catherine and Joanna (see below). He is a staunch supporter of Catholicism, and a personal friend of Grand Inquisitor Diego de Deza.

Rodrigo Díaz de Vivar - More commonly known as "El Cid," meaning 'The Lord' in Arabic. He was a Castilian nobleman and military leader who had lived over 500 years prior to the events in this novel. Christians referred to him as El Campeador which means 'Outstanding Warrior'. He was indeed that, as he fought for both Christians and Muslims during his lifetime. He was a legend in both the collective minds of Europe and the Middle East. He was loved and despised on both sides of the religious divide.

Al Ashraf Qansur al Ghuri, Sultan of the Burji Dynasty - The current Mamluk Sultan in Egypt. The Burji Dynasty, under his rule, is in decline, and this has placed al Ghuri in the difficult position of making desperate moves to thwart the threat of the Ottoman Empire. His eyes are fixed on the Levant as the place in which he will stop the Turkish horde.

Joanna of Castile - Often called Joanna the Mad (Juana la Loca), she is the daughter of King Ferdinand and Queen Isabella, and the sister of Catherine of Aragon. She is a quiet, amorous woman, who spends most of her time dreaming and tending to her flowers. But as she is often fond of saying, 'There is a fine line between madness and ecstatic vision.' There is more to Joanna than meets the eye, and though she is poised to assume the throne of Spain in a few short years, destiny may take her in a different direction.

Factions

Eldar Gods - Nicknamed 'the Dwellers of the Deep' and sometimes 'the Dark Ones', these creatures inhabit the Baltic Ocean and thrust their tentacles up from the sea for one purpose – to destroy humanity and replace them with creatures of their own image. They had once been sealed in a Void by Perun in order to protect humanity, but their battle against the Old Gods has been waged for hundreds of years prior. The only people who have truly seen these creatures have fallen sway to their maniacal whims and have lost all sense of their humanity. Those they have wrapped their tentacles around have clear signs – almonding of the eyes, elongated appendages and craniums, and in some intense cases they begin to grow tentacles of their own as a sign of the power bestowed upon them.

The Spanish Inquisition - Established by King Ferdinand and Queen Isabella in 1478, the Spanish Inquisition's original purpose was to "maintain Catholic orthodoxy" in Spain. Its purpose was to serve Spain and Spain alone, as it represented a break from Papal control and many of the other so-called Inquisitions of the time. But as the threat of the Eldar Gods began to grow in the late 1400s, its purpose grew more focused and by extension, more violent. Now, most people consider The Spanish Inquisition no more than King Ferdinand's hit squad.

Hanseatic League - Once thought to be the world's most elite and elaborate trading organization, their greater purpose and most sacred commodity is secrets. Every member of the guild is trained in the art of swordplay and advanced acrobatics so that they can not only trade valuables across the land, but so that they might spy on the different groups around the realm and adventure to the most desolate ruins to find treasure. They swear allegiance to no overarching group, and even though they fight for the preservation of humanity, their main priority is always protecting their interests and needs above the common man.

Look for more books from Winged Hussar Publishing, LLC – E-books, paperbacks and limited edition hardcovers. The best in history, science fiction and fantasy at:

https://www.wingedhussarpublishing.com

or follow us on Facebook at:

Winged Hussar Publishing LLC

Or on twitter at:

WingHusPubLLC
For information and upcoming publications

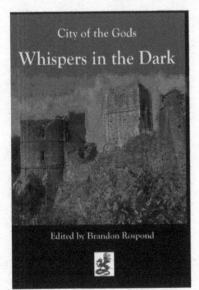